BROKEN PIECES

A TWIST OF FATE

PAYAL PATEL

INDIA · SINGAPORE · MALAYSIA

ISBN
Hardcase 979-8-89588-981-7
Paperback 979-8-89556-381-6

With deepest love and gratitude,
I dedicate this book to my late
mother Hansa, a shining example of
kindness and compassion.

CONTENTS

Contents

PREFACE

I am forever grateful to two individuals who helped me discover my true potential. If not for their guidance and support, I may have never uncovered my talent. First and foremost, I want to express my heartfelt thanks to my sister-in-law, Hiral Patel, who changed my life and showed me a new direction. Her influence helped me connect with my inner self and tap into my creativity, and I will always be thankful for her presence in my life. Secondly, I deeply thank my husband, Nishant Bhanderi, whose unwavering support and encouragement have nurtured my writing journey. He introduced me to the Pratilipi platform where I began expressing my thoughts through short stories and series. His recognition of my creative potential and persistent encouragement have empowered me to grow as a writer. Thank you, Nishant, for believing in me and helping me unlock my full potential.

I'd also like to express my heartfelt appreciation to my brother, Sanjay Patel, for being a constant presence in my life. The bond between siblings is truly special, and I'm grateful for the laughter, tears, and memories we've shared. Even though we've had our share of fights and disagreements, his love and support have always been a source of comfort. Thank you, brother, for being there for me through all the ups and downs. Your presence means the world to me.

Surrounded by three tiny bundles of joy - my nieces, Neeraja Patel and Yutika Patel, and my son, Sattva - I'm constantly reminded of life's beauty, wonder, and magic. Their bright smiles and contagious laughter lift my spirits on even the toughest days. I'm grateful to learn from them every day and thankful for the love and light they bring to my world. Thank you, my little titans, for being my sunshine!

I thank the Universe for sending Devendra Gautam, a celebrated author, who helped me find my identity and purpose. His mentorship and encouragement have been instrumental in my journey. I'm grateful for his support, which has enabled me to take significant strides in my writing career. Thank you, Devendraji, for believing in me.

I'm deeply thankful for the remarkable individuals who have been my pillars of support – Khushbu Mangrolia, Jigar Parmar, Deepti Thakkar, Bhautik Patel, Nisarg Patel, Ritesh Patel, Bhavesh Vaghela, Ayudh Panchal, Rupa Siddhpur, Kevin sir, and Hetal Patel. Your unwavering support, unshakeable faith, and invaluable guidance have been my anchor, my motivation, and my strength. You're more than just friends, mentors, and family - you're my lifeline. Your unwavering belief in me, your guidance, and your friendship have made all the difference, enabling me to persevere, grow, and thrive. Thank you for being my rock, my safe haven, and my forever friends. Thank you for being my constant source of inspiration, comfort, and joy.

Wishing my readers a delightful and enriching experience with my book. May it bring joy and inspiration to your lives. Happy Reading!

GLANCE

The light scattered everywhere, casting a warm and festive glow over the wedding celebration. The incorporation of technology, particularly drones, has revolutionized the field of videography and photography, capturing breathtaking views and moments. Meanwhile, relatives chatted and mingled, while children bounced around energetically, and some even practiced their dance moves. In addition, others engaged in lively conversations or greeted arriving guests. One of the most special aspects of a wedding is when everyone dons traditional attire, creating a unique and unforgettable atmosphere. Laughter echoed from every corner, adding to the excitement and joy of the occasion.

I couldn't believe I was finally seeing my friends after several years apart. "It's nice to meet familiar faces among strangers after 5 years... don't you feel the same?" I asked Ethan and smiled genuinely.

"Yes... Honestly, I had been looking forward to this day, hoping something would bring us together. We weren't even together on our last day of college. Life has been so materialistic; I can hardly believe how quickly these five years have flown by!" Ethan sighed.

"Life is so materialistic these days, bro!" I said, patting his shoulder. He nodded in agreement.

Hazel chimed in, "These are just excuses... we all know the truth. Everyone knows lies can never be veiled. Don't use a busy schedule as a false excuse. The real question is why none of us bothered to make a phone call or send a text message... I suppose we all know the answer."

I kept silent for a while. Finally, Ethan broke the ice, "Oh, wow! Congratulations on becoming a lawyer! If I ever have a case in court, I'll come to you for help."

Hazel rolled her eyes, "Shut up!"

Ethan continued, "Hey, my dear detective Hezu!! I missed you the most!" He pinched her cheeks, and his enthusiasm was evident.

Hazel retorted, "Why can't you stop mocking me? Maybe it's because nothing has changed over these years, which might be why you don't have a girlfriend."

I chuckled at their banter.

Ethan winked at Hazel, "I don't tolerate nonsense... and honestly, you're more than enough for me!"

Hazel raised an eyebrow and rolled her eyes, "Forgive me. I forgot that you are sitting here."

Their dynamic was more complex than a simple rivalry; there was an undeniable friendship even amidst their frequent squabbles. Ethan's relentless teasing of Hazel, a habit formed in college and had become a familiar spectacle. His quick wit and sarcasm often left others bewildered, earning him a reputation for mischief. Despite this, Ethan and Hazel's relationship was more nuanced than a simple game of cat and mouse. Beneath their constant bickering lay a deep-seated camaraderie, a testament to their enduring friendship. Hazel, no stranger to cleverness herself, frequently turned the tables on Ethan, employing her keen detective skills to outmaneuver him - and everyone else - with ease.

Rakshit greeted us with a smile, dressed in a pearl grey Indo-Western kurta, paired with an off-white salwar. The diamond brooch on his kurta added a touch of elegance.

Ethan teased, "Seeing you, I feel like you are a king! Well, I have to say that you are looking damn charming in this outfit. I have a question... Why did you choose Jaipur for your wedding?"

Rakshit smiled subtly, "I have many fond memories associated with this place!"

Hazel shifted the topic, "I can hardly believe you're actually getting married!"

Ethan sarcastically remarked, "Detectives might feel frustrated because they lack gadgets to determine if someone is content in their marriage. What do you think, Hezal?"

Hazel retorted, "I think I should punch your face. Why don't you keep your nose out of my business? I guess interruption has become your hobby!"

Rakshit asked, perplexed, "It's been so many years, and you two still haven't changed? Aren't you both tired of it by now?"

I asked Rakshit, "I don't think so. Let them be… When will your dance performance be?"

Rakshit smiled, "I am waiting for someone!"

Ethan curiously asked, "Is that person he or she?"

"Why not just ask if the person is a girl?" Hazel suggested.

Ethan quipped, "Should I give you a certificate for your intelligence?"

Rakshit pointed to the gate, " Don't fight. The person I'm referring to has just arrived. Look over there."

Hazel said curiously, "Ahana!!"

Rakshit immediately approached Ahana and embraced her warmly. Ethan and Hazel also went to greet her, but I stood frozen, unsure of what to do. My mind raced, questioning whether I should go see her. As soon as I heard her name, my heartbeat quickened.

"What is she doing here?" I asked, pretending to be arrogant.

Ethan replied with a naughty smile, "She is our friend too. Since when have you started to forget?"

Hazel scold, "Please try not to create any scenes over here."

I looked at Hazel, "Why are you scolding me? You know the reason very well!"

Hazel said confidently, "We all know the facts, and deep down, you know you're not entirely right!"

I asked, "Whose side are you on? Mine or hers?"

Hazel replied, her voice tinged with irritation, "I'm not here to choose sides or take sides. I'm here to attend my friend's wedding. Please forgive me and don't involve me in this."

Rakshit called out loudly, "Guys, come over here... let's dance!"

Ethan enthusiastically said, "It's time to play some games in musical events... after all, we all are meeting with each other after a long time!"

I said without looking at Ahana, "I don't trust her. Save your enthusiasm, because you know how she is. Later on, you will need this energy to clean the mess."

Hazel said with a cold tone, "Yours or hers? How long will you take those things in your heart? It's been five years, Vihan!!"

Ethan intervened, "It's okay. Let's drop it for now. This isn't the right moment to discuss it. We'll talk about it later. For now, let's just enjoy the event!"

As the event went on, we all had a great time together, and my expectations about Ahana were turning out to be wrong. I had anticipated she would be yelling at me or causing a scene in the middle of the event, but none of that happened. She didn't even glance my way. Laughter and music filled the air as we danced and celebrated Rakshit's special day. I couldn't help but sneak glances at Ahana, who seemed to be enjoying herself, chatting with Hazel and Ethan. She looked different and more refined, and her dimpled smile captivated me.

As the night wore on, Ethan pulled me into the festivities, and I found myself having a great time, despite my initial reservations. Ahana's presence still lingered in my mind, but I tried to push the thoughts aside and focus on the celebration.

Rakshit's voice boomed through the microphone, "It's time for the final performance! Please welcome Ahana on stage!"

My heart skipped a beat as Ahana walked onto the stage, her eyes sparkling under the bright lights. She began to sing, her voice melodious and soulful, captivating the entire audience. I couldn't take my eyes off her, mesmerized by her performance. For a moment, the past seemed to fade away, and all that mattered was the present. As Ahana finished her song, the crowd erupted into applause, cheering and whistling.

Ethan announced, "And now, it's time for the final dance performance! Please welcome the bride and groom on stage!"

The music began, and Rakshit and his bride took to the stage, dancing gracefully together.

Ahana joined in, and soon everyone was dancing, immersed in the joy of the moment. As I glanced at Ahana in silence, a strange sense of peace settled in my heart.

LAW OF ATTRACTION

I saw Ahana after five years. Considering everything that had happened that day, I hadn't taken a good look at her. Over time, I had come to dislike her voice. But seeing her again after all these years made me question whether my anger toward her was truly justified.

Her face kept flashing in front of my eyes. Even though I had only seen her briefly last night, that fleeting encounter seemed to have left an indelible mark on my heart. My thoughts were constantly drawn to her, despite my efforts to push them aside. Around me, everyone was laughing, talking, and gossiping, but I was lost in my own world.

I was lost in my thoughts when I suddenly noticed her. Even today, she looks stunning. I couldn't tell if her beauty was due to her attire or if she had simply grown more radiant over the years. She wore a plain green lehenga, simple and unadorned, but it was striking in its simplicity. The white scarf she draped over her shoulders had delicate handwork along the edges that complemented the lehenga perfectly. She wore no jewellery except for earrings, yet her presence was captivating.

"It's not my cup of tea!" Ahana said joyfully.

"Why not? And by the way, why tea? Why not coffee?" Ethan asked, clearly excited.

"It's a idiom, you bozo!" Hazel said with a taunt.

"Oh, thank you! If you hadn't mentioned it, I would never have known!" Ethan said sarcastically and laughed, and everybody joined.

"Why do you keep harassing her?" Ahana asked Ethan.

"If she comes to me on her own and knocks on my door, what should I do? You know I never turn away anyone who asks for help!" Ethan said with a wink at Ahana.

"I don't think you'll ever change!" Hazel said furiously.

"Of course not, baby. By the way, Rakshit, now you are out of our community, from today onwards." Ethan said with a naughty smile.

"Why so? What crime have I committed? And which community are you talking about?" Rakshit asked surprisingly.

"It's simple. You're the first among us to get married, so in just a few hours, you'll officially be 'Married. That means you'll no longer be part of the 'Singles' or 'Bachelors' club. Am I right, everyone?" Ethan said with confidence.

"Don't take it the wrong way, Rakshit, but there's actually a point to his rambling!" Ahana said, raising an eyebrow.

"Rakshit... come over here, beta." Rakshit's mother said.

"I have to go, but you guys enjoy!" Rakshit said and left.

"Looks like Rakshit is about to be the scapegoat!" Ethan said with a laugh.

"What is the matter with you? You look damn happy today!!" Ahana asked.

"I don't understand why people get jealous of others' happiness!" I remarked, and the room fell silent for a full two minutes. Ethan and Hazel stared at me as though I'd committed a crime, but Ahana didn't even glance in my direction.

Finally, Hazel broke the silence. "So, Ahana, when are you heading back? Rakshit mentioned that because of his wedding, you stayed and might not find a flight for the next two weeks."

"Some people just seem destined for bad luck!" I muttered. Hazel and Ethan gave me looks that could have pierced through stone.

"Umm… I need to make an important call. Please excuse me!" Ahana said, leaving without meeting my gaze.

"I'll go after her. And you—watch your words before you speak, Vihan." Ethan scolded me. I was also fuming and about to stand up, but Hazel stopped me.

"Whoa… hey, where are you going? Come over here and sit." Hazel said, pretty mad at me.

"What? Are you going to lecture me?" I asked, exhaling in frustration.

"Yes, it seems like it. Ever since she arrived, you've been harassing and torturing her. Can't you see that she hasn't mentioned you and isn't even looking at you? After all these years, you should understand that what happened wasn't Ahana's fault—it was just an accident. It's in the past, and she's trying to move on. Don't hurt her any further. She's stayed here knowing you're around, and if she's behaving normally, why can't you? Leave her alone. She's not the bandage for your wound, Vihan."

"I'm not intentionally causing any problems; I truly don't want her to be upset with me. I also want to enjoy our time together since we're all reconnecting after many years through this marriage. I don't want to make a scene, but I struggle to find the right words whenever she's around. I often say things I didn't mean, which unintentionally hurts her. Believe it or not, I really don't want to hurt her—I'm just feeling confused myself." I sighed.

"Ohh... hahaha... The Law of Attraction! I hope you figure it out soon; the sooner you understand it, the better for you. First...get yourself together, and then we can have a proper discussion about it." Hazel said with a sarcastic smile before walking away.

Hazel's words felt like a puzzle to me. Those three words—Law of Attraction—were troubling me deeply. I was already preoccupied with thoughts about Ahana, and now I had to contend with this unfamiliar concept. What exactly was the Law of Attraction?

I was lost in my thoughts when Ethan returned, looking concerned. "Vihan, I think you should take a walk or something. You're getting worked up over nothing."

I nodded, knowing he was right. I needed some fresh air to clear my head.

As I stepped outside, I couldn't shake off the feeling that Ahana's presence had stirred up. I felt like I was torn between my heart and mind, unsure of what to do next. I took a deep breath, trying to calm myself down. But the questions lingered: What was the Law of Attraction? And how did it relate to my situation with Ahana?

SLEEPING BEAUTY

Whatever Hazel had said yesterday was spreading through my mind like a virus. I didn't fully understand everything, but it seemed like I had feelings for Ahana. I found myself bombarded with a thousand questions. Was I still feeling something for Ahana? Did my heart still hold feelings for her? When did my heart start to fall for her? Was it attraction or love? Should I just forget what happened five years ago?

After a while, I wondered if I should even be paying attention to these questions. I felt a sense of relief in her presence, so why was I still stuck in the past? My mind was swirling with confusion and unanswered questions about Hazel's comments.

The Haldi ceremony was in full swing. Rakshit appeared a lively shade of pale yellow. Whoever invented these wedding ceremonies in our country made a brilliant discovery! Each ritual comes with its own unique style and significance.

We were all busy taking selfies and group photos with Rakshit, but my mind was elsewhere. My focus was completely off; I was interacting with everyone, yet I had no idea what I was actually saying.

Everyone was there except Ahana. I felt strangely unsettled, having not seen her since the morning. Her absence was stirring up a whirlwind of thoughts. My mind was once again flooded with questions: Had my behaviour yesterday been so awful that it upset her? Had I hurt her in some way? What could be the reason for her absence? My thoughts were racing like a game show quiz, constantly throwing questions at me. I struggled to concentrate on what everyone was saying, my eyes constantly searching for a glimpse of her.

"Sleeping Beauty!" Hazel whispered in my ear.

"What?" I asked, surprised.

"She's sleeping peacefully." Hazel chuckled.

"What are you talking about?" I asked, puzzled.

"Really? Then why are you looking around so much? Has Rakshit hired you as his bodyguard?" Hazel teased, giggling and raising an eyebrow.

"What are you two talking about? That's not fair! Gossiping isn't allowed when you're with your friends!" Ethan said, scolding them.

"We're not gossiping. I'm just teasing him." Hazel replied with a laugh.

"You can't steal my thing from me. How dare you try to take my identity?" Ethan challenged.

"What on earth are you talking about, you idiot?" Hazel said, clearly enraged.

"Sarcasm and teasing are my specialities, I won't deny that it's part of my identity. You're trying to snatch it away from me! I thought you were my friend, but now you're betraying me!" Ethan said, shaking his head.

"Hell with your identity! I have no interest in your meaningless claims. I have my own identity." Hazel said, raising her voice.

"Which one? The 'Inevitable Detective' or the 'Useless Detective'?" Ethan retorted, laughing.

"Hey! Enough already! I don't know how we managed both of you during college. You both are roasting each other all the time!" I said with a heavy sigh.

"What's going on here?" Rakshit asked, Along with his face, his kurta was smeared with turmeric. His hair had a turmeric tint as well, yet looked great.

"Hazel's been teasing Vihan... Nothing much." Ethan said with a chuckle.

"Ahana isn't here, so how did that happen?" Rakshit asked, laughing. Everyone joined in, except for me.

"His situation is more dramatic than a soap opera. Let him be." Hazel said, patting my back.

"Why? What happened?" Rakshit asked.

"Nothing. I'll fill you in if I get a chance!" Hazel replied.

"Sure. Anyway, when did she go to sleep?" Rakshit asked Hazel. I was puzzled as to why he asked Hazel about Ahana's sleep schedule.

"She went to bed around 4 in the morning!" Hazel replied.

"What was she doing until then?" I asked, unable to hide my anxiety.

"She stayed up late. She had some office work that needed to be finished." Hazel explained.

Rakshit and Ethan exchanged amused glances and chuckled.

"I'm just asking out of curiosity!" I said, feeling defensive.

"None of us are asking you anything. Why are you explaining?" Rakshit said, giving me a wink. Hazel and Ethan burst into laughter. I felt utterly miserable and, for the first time, I pitied myself.

"Don't worry. I should probably explain. She stayed up because of me. Now, her office work had to be finished in this way. I felt a strange happiness seeing her after so many years. I never imagined she would learn to live independently like this...all alone!" Rakshit said with a sigh.

"It's true, but she has a remarkable ability to turn strangers into friends. That's her greatest strength! Back in college, she was the only one who could challenge me equally. It was really nice to see her. I never thought she'd come to any of our weddings." Ethan said with a smile.

"I felt the same. At first, she turned me down, but I was able to persuade her in the end. I considered her more like a sister than just a friend and I'm glad that she came." Rakshit said.

"I'll be back. I just remembered some important work... I need to do." I said and quickly left.

I couldn't stop myself from wanting to see her. My feet seemed to move on their own towards her room. Rakshit's destination wedding was in Jaipur and everyone had their own rooms, so I knew Ahana was staying in Hazel's room.

When I reached her door, I spotted Ahana through the window. I didn't want to disturb her sleep, so I remained outside, trying to catch a glimpse through the window. Even while asleep, she looked as beautiful as ever, without makeup. Her hair was splayed across her face, yet she slept peacefully as if it didn't bother her at all. The serenity on her face was calming, and I wanted to keep watching her. Seeing her sleep so serenely gave my heart an unexpected sense of relief. "She looks cute while sleeping!!" I muttered.

"I didn't realize it was part of your important job to watch Ahana sleep!" Hazel said, chuckling softly.

"You scared me!" I replied with a heavy sigh.

"People's breath gets caught like this when they're caught red-handed!" Hazel teased.

"Shut up. Are you playing a 'Peek-a-boo' game with me?" I asked.

"No, but if you let me, I'd love to. Such opportunities don't come around often. It will evoke some memories of my childhood!" Hazel said, winking at me.

"Just don't tell anyone about this." I requested.

"Believe me, I'm very good at keeping everyone's secrets! And I agree—she looks cute while sleeping." Hazel said.

"Hey! You're seriously unbelievable!" I said, astonished.

"I know…Anyway, come on. We need to talk now!" she said.

"About what?" I asked, puzzled.

"About Ahana, you idiot!" Hazel replied. She grabbed my hand and led me away. These days, I didn't dare to win an argument with Hazel!

EGO

Hazel leading me by the hand made me feel like a child again! Thankfully, no one was watching us. I had no idea what she wanted to discuss, and though I didn't want to think about anything, my mind was racing. I was following Hazel, lost in my thoughts, when she suddenly stopped, causing me to bump into her.

"Ouch! What the hell are you doing? Where were you lost?" Hazel asked, a bit annoyed.

"Nowhere!" I replied casually.

"Oh, of course. It wasn't me you were following—someone else bumped into me!" she said, raising an eyebrow.

"I'm sorry. Are you okay? Did I hurt you?" I asked.

"Thank you for asking. Anyway, I've explained it before and am still explaining: please think it over carefully!" Hazel said seriously.

"What are you talking about? I don't understand anything. Just say what you need to say clearly. I don't like puzzles." I said.

"I just want to say that the mistake from five years ago shouldn't be repeated. That incident changed everything for us. You might have lost your loved one on that day, but we all lost our friendship because of it. If you think about it, even now we're all distant. We're only here because of Rakshit's wedding—otherwise, I don't think any of us would have come together again. Ahana used to enjoy spending time with us when you weren't around, and now it seems you're doing the same thing she did. Do you genuinely believe Ahana was at fault for what happened?" Hazel paused for a moment, then continued.

"I know it's better to forget the past, especially the painful parts. But even our bitter memories have their place, and Ahana is tied to them. Our good and bad memories are intertwined with her, especially yours. Everyone shut away those memories after that day, but I don't want to relive those same painful days. I'm asking you to think carefully about your actions from now on because I can't bear to lose either of you again," Hazel said, her eyes filled with tears.

"To be honest, after all these years, I've come to realize that she really wasn't at fault. When I was alone, I'd reflect on it and realize that I was more to blame than she was. Even though I knew the truth, I could never bring myself to admit it to her—or anyone else. I don't know why. After she left, I understood how deeply I had missed her and what she truly meant to me. It felt like I lost all of you with her. You're right—although we're all together now, it doesn't feel like we're really connected. I want to be around her, but I can't. I want to talk to her, but I can't. I want to see her, but I can't... I don't understand what's happening to me." I said with a heavy sigh.

"EGO. It's your ego." Hazel said.

"What?" I asked, surprised.

"Don't be so surprised. The struggle you're feeling isn't really about her; it's about your ego. Your heart wants to move on and have her back in your life, but your mind holds you back because it values its own pride. Don't let your mind overpower your heart. If you let ego take over love, where will love have room to grow?" she said gently.

"It's not that simple. I just don't understand what's happening to me!" I said.

"I've said what I needed to. I hope you realize soon that you're trapped in your own ego. Think about it, Vihan—she wasn't even going to come here, but she did, and now her flight is two weeks away. Luck doesn't offer everyone a second chance, but you've been given one. So, recognize it and put your pride aside," Hazel said.

"How likely is it that she'd be willing to talk to me after knowing all this, even if I set my ego aside?" I asked.

"It depends on you. If you truly love her, you'll know who really matters. True love doesn't need proof; Ahana will understand if your feelings are genuine." Hazel said.

"Hold on a second, How did you know I loved her? I thought Rakshit was the only one who knew about it." I asked perplexedly.

"Everyone knows, you goof. Even she knew about your feelings towards her." Hazel said with a chuckle.

"What? How can I even bring myself to talk to her now?" I said.

"I thought you knew her nature better than her!" Hazel taunted.

I know Ahana, but this new version of her scares me a little." I admitted.

"Thank you for acknowledging that. And by the way, she doesn't have a new version." Hazel said as she started to walk away.

"Hey, where are you going?" I called after her.

"If you give yourself some time, you might start to understand what's really going on inside you. I should probably go now. I need to wake Ahana up so she doesn't miss today's function. Meanwhile, just think things through. Remember, you've seen her after five years, so it's possible that what you're feeling could just be the attraction. It's important to distinguish between love and attraction if that's the case." Hazel said.

"Are you advising me or just confusing me?" I asked, feeling perplexed.

"Haha ... This is just the beginning!! When you start thinking about it, you'll probably end up even more confused than I am. Trust me. Honestly, I'd be thrilled if you made the right decision. Enjoy your 'me time' and take your time to figure things out. Don't rush it. I hope you understand what I mean. Take care." She said and walked away.

One question kept repeating in my mind: is this the same Hazel I knew back in college? I couldn't believe how much she had changed and grown. Her words had a profound impact on me, causing me to lose awareness of everything else for a few minutes.

HIDE AND SEEK

Hazel's words lingered in my mind, only adding to my confusion. I spent the entire day grappling with what I truly wanted in the end. Since our last day of college, I've felt her absence acutely and gradually realized that I could never love anyone but Ahana. They say ego can shatter a person, and that's exactly what happened to me. I couldn't pinpoint what I wanted from Hazel, even though Ahana had done everything possible. Despite her efforts, I failed to see her clearly. Maybe Hazel was right— ego involved, and it might have cost me Ahana. Today, after all these years, seeing her again brought a whirlwind of emotions: anger, hatred, love, and pain, all mingling and trapping me in a storm of confusion.

All day, I struggled with my ego, longing for Ahana to come back into my life. I remembered my grandmother's advice: if someone is truly worth having in your life, you must set aside all anger, hatred, and especially ego to reach out to them. I didn't understand her words at the time, as my ego was overpowering me. My five years of ego proved stronger than my three years of love. Ahana endured my bitterness far more than my affection. Even now, she endures my taunts in silence, never responding or even looking at me. What could be a harsher punishment for me than that? I wish I could have understood her love better.

Hazel was right; she made me think outside the box. I love Ahana, but my ego has been in the way. Maybe that's why I've been trapped between love and attraction. Despite all the trouble I caused her, she continued to plead for our love. I should have recognized her feelings, especially since I loved her too. The incident left me so emotionally shattered that I couldn't see clearly. Hazel was right—life doesn't always offer second chances, and if I've been given one, I need to make the most of it. I tried dating other women, but Ahana's face never left my mind. There were many times I wanted to hear her voice but hesitated, held back by my ego.

My heart was in such turmoil that I couldn't make sense of it. There was a time when I would approach her with reckless abandon, but now I found myself terrified to even be near her. Whenever I caught sight of her, I'd try to hide, my entire body seized with anxiety, my shivering and goosebumps more intense than ever before. This had never happened to me until today. Though it was oddly reassuring to watch her from afar and see her smile, I realized today just how intense the fever of love can be. I found myself grinning despite the turmoil.

"May I join you?" Hazel asked with a chuckle.

"Hey! Could you stop playing games with me? You really scared me!" I replied, catching my breath.

"Aww, sorry! But you're my favourite player in this game—at least for now!" she said, bursting into laughter.

"Whatever and what game are you talking about?" I asked, puzzled.

"Hide and seek!" Hazel said, smiling anxiously.

"Who's playing?" I asked, still surprised.

"Of course, you are! I've noticed you sneaking around when Ahana's around, so I figured you might be playing hide and seek!" she said, her tone dripping with sarcasm.

"When is your inner detective going to take a break? Ever since college, it's like I've been dealing with Sherlock Holmes. Tell him to give it a rest and let you be yourself!" I said, raising an eyebrow.

"I don't think he'll be going anywhere anytime soon. He helps me catch people like you red-handed...but seriously, why are you hiding?" Hazel said.

"I don't know. Whenever I see her, my heart races so fast it feels like everyone around can hear it. I've tried countless times to approach her, but I just can't bring myself to do it. It's as if my body goes numb every time I look at her. When she heads in my direction, I instinctively change course. I don't want to cause her any more pain, so I try to keep my distance. But tell me, how did you find the time to notice all of this?" I asked.

"Does it really matter? What matters is that you're falling in love with her again!" Hazel said with a playful wink.

"What?" I replied, shocked.

"Don't drag this out. Just admit it!" Hazel said.

"This is too much! Were you always like this, or have you changed over these five years?" I asked.

"Didn't I warn both of you that gossiping isn't allowed without me? What's with you two? And why are you smiling like that, Hazel?" Ethan interjected.

"It's my choice. Do you have a problem with it?" Hazel shot back.

"She gets drunk easily, don't let her drink. Didn't I warn you about that, too?" Ethan said, chuckling.

"Shut up. Can't you find someone else to bother?" Hazel said, clearly irritated.

"Stop it! Can you two never have a peaceful conversation?" I said, frustrated. "Anyway, let's go."

We arrived at the table where Ahana and Rakshit were sitting.

"I've been looking for all of you. Where have you been?" Rakshit asked.

"Ask them. These two have betrayed us and conspired together." Ethan said, pointing at Hazel and me.

"What nonsense you are talking about? Just because you're not aware of our conversation doesn't mean you should assume things! I didn't realize you had also mastered the art of playing tricks on us." I defended.

"Ahana, you know him well. You used to catch his lies easily before, so do the same today!" Ethan said. Everyone, except Ahana, turned their attention to him.

"You're being a bit ridiculous sometimes!" Hazel said, scolding him.

"He didn't say anything wrong. Just because of the past doesn't mean you should keep holding onto it. What's done is done, and no one can change that. But that doesn't mean you can't talk about it. It's not right to suppress it. Those were our memories, and they will remain with us forever, whether they're good or bad. We're all part of those memories. From now on, let's not try to control or erase them by recalling them!" Ahana said with a smile.

I couldn't believe she said that! Even though she was the most hurt, she smiled and allowed the old discussions to continue.

"So, can I call you 'jangli billi' now?" Ethan asked, and everyone burst into laughter.

For the first time, it felt like her laughter was unrestrained. Her laughter transported me to the day, I first met her at the freshers' party. That was our first encounter.

BACK TO COLLEGE LIFE

Freshers Party

"The exams are approaching, and they're throwing us a freshers' party!" Hazel said with exhaustion.

Indian Institutes of Technology (IITs) are renowned for their excellence, and I've been admitted to the IIT in Jaipur, which ranks among the top ten engineering institutes in India. IITs receive significantly higher funding compared to other engineering colleges in the country. They offer comprehensive on-campus residential facilities for students, research scholars, and faculty. Additionally, IITs are equipped with sports grounds for basketball, cricket, football (soccer), hockey, volleyball, lawn tennis, badminton, and athletics, as well as swimming pools for aquatic events. These institutions are often seen as a paradise for students, which is why gaining admission is incredibly competitive.

The attractive salary packages offered during campus interviews further enhance the appeal of these colleges, promising a bright future for graduates.

After arriving at this college, I realized that the real hard work was just beginning. It turned out that it wasn't the paradise it initially seemed to be. Most of my time was consumed by studies, leaving little room for anything else, though we boys managed to carve out some time for ourselves. Here, I became friends with Ethan, Rakshit, and Hazel. Hazel was the only girl in our group, and she definitely had a dominant presence. Ethan was the one who could keep her in check. Hazel's detective-like mind made our lives quite challenging!

"Relax, we still have a month left. If you stress out this much, how will you enjoy life? Feel free to join the party if you want, but if not, just keep quiet and stop distracting me with exam talk. Don't you know, there will be some beautiful girls there?" Ethan said.

This was our first college party. Loudspeakers were set up in each corner of the hall, and everyone was dancing. Some boys were dressed in formal attire, others in casual clothes, and a few in stylish outfits. The girls' outfits are always beyond my understanding, all the girls wore a variety of dresses as if they were all ready to compete for the Miss Universe crown this night. We boys usually take a relaxed approach to parties, with our main goal being to "eat, drink, and have fun." We don't pay much attention to the decorations; our focus is always on the food and drinks. This party was no exception—I might not have known about the decorations, but there was certainly no shortage of food and mocktails.

"Don't say anything. You've already studied almost everything and just need to review. And those hot chicks? They're probably out of your league—they're likely seniors." Hazel said.

"So what? Let me enjoy myself. Don't bother me!" Ethan said, turning his attention back to the girls.

"Leave him alone. Why are you so worked up? Oh, and by the way, you could have finished your studying too, but you were too busy watching Sherlock Holmes. How could you find time to study?" I said sarcastically.

"Don't say anything about that. I enjoy watching it—the new mysteries, the cases, the suspense, those thrilling vibes... That's what makes it so great. Only someone with a keen mind can appreciate it, which you clearly don't, so... just stay out of it!" Hazel said, her voice tinged with pride.

"Yes, of course. You're the only one with a sharp mind, which is why we all hang out with you—so you can save us if anything goes wrong!" Ethan replied, and we all laughed.

"Whenever the topic is about me, you all get so distracted! Why is that?" Hazel said, clearly irritated.

"It's not that important, but look over there! See that girl? She's giving that poor boy a hard time!" Ethan said, pointing at a boy standing in the corner.

"Oh, that's Ahana. I heard she's new here because her parents transferred, but she prefers to stay in the hostel. She's quiet, but her eyes say a lot. Her heart is pure, but if anyone teases her, she's as fierce as a cobra!" Rakshit said, and we all looked at him in surprise.

"How do you know so much about her? When did you become an expert at reading people's eyes? Tell me, what do my eyes say?" Ethan asked with a chuckle.

"It's not like that. I've met her a couple of times. She was very kind and even helped me with a query." Rakshit explained.

"Can I ask when all this happened?" Ethan said and raised his eyebrow.

"Didn't Hazel tell you anything? She's become good friends with her!" Rakshit said. Ethan and I both turned to look at Hazel, our faces filled with questions and surprise.

"Don't look at me like that. I figured neither of you was interested in hearing about newcomers, so I didn't mention it!" Hazel said defensively.

"I expected this from you. Keep her out of my sight—she's a traitor!" Ethan said.

"Stop the drama. I can introduce her if you want!" Hazel said, a hint of envy in her voice.

"Why seek permission from someone you're doing a favour for?" Ethan asked, curious.

Hazel went over and began talking to her. After a while, both of them approached us. This was my first meeting with Ahana at the party, and she made quite an impression. She wore blue jeans and a grey long-sleeve T-shirt, with no makeup... looking effortlessly simple. Yet, she seemed to be the most beautiful girl at the party. Perhaps it was her flowing hair that contributed to her charm. For some reason, Her presence filled me with an overwhelming sense of pleasure. I found myself captivated by her for a moment.

"Stop staring like that. If you keep looking at her, how am I supposed to get a chance to talk?" Ethan whispered in my ear.

"It's not like that. Her face is just comforting." I said with a smile. From the way Ethan looked at me, I could tell he didn't quite get it.

"Hey, guys! Meet my friend, Ahana!" Hazel announced. We all greeted her, shaking hands one by one.

"Let me guess—you must be Ethan! The one who always enjoys teasing others and has a knack for witty comebacks. Your signature move is sarcasm, and people often call you the 'King of

Sarcasm.' Am I right?" Ahana said, raising an eyebrow.

"Tell me the truth, who are you? How do you know so much about me? Have you been keeping an eye on me? Do you like me that much?" Ethan asked with a wink.

"Hazel was right—you're such a drama king. Everything I've heard about you seems to be true!" Ahana said with a smile, clearly amused by Ethan's sarcasm.

"If you keep this up, how will any girl ever want to be with me? Snitcher!" Ethan said to Hazel.

"Honestly, I'm saving the girls from you because you don't know how to talk straightforwardly, and I doubt they'd appreciate your cheesy jokes. You should thank me instead of blaming me!" Hazel replied.

"Enough already. Can't you two ever stop arguing?" Rakshit said.

"Don't worry about it. I'll just start teasing Ahana instead of Hazel now." Ethan said, winking at Ahana.

"In your dreams—because that'll never happen in real life, so don't get your hopes up, baby!" Ahana said confidently, raising her eyebrow. For some reason, I found myself enjoying every moment of her demeanour.

"Now this should be interesting. At least someone is giving you a fitting reply!" Rakshit said with a grin. "By the way, Ahana, this is Vihan!" he gestured towards me.

"Hey!" Ahana said with a smile.

"'Hey'? That's it? Aren't you going to say something interesting about me, like you did with Ethan?" I asked, surprised.

"What do you think? Am I an astrologer? I'm not here for entertainment. Plus, it's not necessary to say something about everyone. I know what to say to whom?" Ahana replied.

"You're like a 'Jangli billi'—you don't hesitate to reply to anyone!" Ethan said with a chuckle.

"I'm sorry, but I've never heard of wild cats responding in that way; they're only known for their attacks. I think you might have the wrong phrase!" Ahana said with a smirk.

"Who cares about the phrase or what I've heard? You're just that girl who doesn't hesitate to answer anyone. So, in my book, you're a 'jangli billi!'" Ethan said, looking at Ahana with his slightly tipsy gaze.

"I'll take that as a compliment! I'm enjoying these little jokes, but I have to go now. See you tomorrow, Mr. Trickster!" Ahana said with a smile just before she left.

For the first time, I felt a pang of jealousy towards Ethan. He had the chance to talk to Ahana, while I was left on the sidelines. I also wanted to talk to her, but she was entirely engrossed in Ethan's antics. There was something about her that intrigued me—something that set her apart from everyone else. It wasn't that she looked like an angel or a nymph, but her unique style captivated me. I had never thought of a girl in this way before. I didn't understand what was happening, but my heart ached to meet her again. My focus on the party was lost; Ahana had taken all my attention.

BIODATA MEETING

The next morning, I was waiting on the college campus, eager to see Ahana. I couldn't quite understand why I felt such a strong urge to talk to her and learn more about her. There was something uniquely compelling about her that occupied my thoughts. I hadn't slept well the previous night, feeling restless and uneasy, as if my encounter with Ahana was to blame. Although she had spoken to everyone else, she hadn't interacted much with me, and that left me curious and drawn to her.

Lost in my thoughts, I suddenly spotted her. She looked quite different today! Perhaps I hadn't recognized her in a salwar kameez after seeing her in jeans the day before. She wore a green kameez with a white salwar, and a printed white dupatta draped over one shoulder. Her hair was left loose, and besides a watch on her left wrist... she wore no other accessories. A black rubber band was on her right wrist, and she had wireless earbuds in her ears, waving her hands in the air as if she were alone and carefree.

"Hi!" I said with a smile.

"Gosh, you scared me!" she replied, catching her breath.

"If you stay lost in your world, this is bound to happen!" I said.

"I didn't know my world would have stalkers like you. Otherwise, I might have chosen a different one!" she said, rolling her eyes. I felt like she didn't like my presence.

"Are you mad at me?" I asked.

"I have no such business with you!" she replied promptly.

"Then why do you call me a stalker?" I asked, starting to walk alongside her.

"If you're not a stalker, then... what are you doing here?" she asked.

"Can't I even talk to you?" I said.

"In return for a question, there should be answers, not more questions. Don't you know that? Anyway, I'm not your friend, so you won't get any answers from me. Essentially, you're neither a friend nor someone important to me—you're just a stranger. So why would I talk to you?" she said.

"Hey! Have you forgotten me? We met just yesterday at the party!" I said, surprised.

"Of course, I remember. Your name is Vihan, and you're Hazel's friend. We met at the party, but just one meeting isn't enough to decide we're friends. I met many other people like you at the party last night, but that doesn't mean I Should count them as friends." She replied.

"You're pretty tough. I like your attitude...if we start talking, we'll gradually become friends. I'll tell you about myself, and you can do the same. So, tell me—where are you from? How many people are in your family? What are your interests? What is your ambition, and so on?" I said.

"Easy there! Don't make me feel like I've come to a marriage bureau to give my biodata. I value my freedom, and why would I be interested in sharing all my personal details with you?" she asked, sitting down on a bench.

"I'm not giving up that easily. I'm determined to be your friend. I like you, and that's why I won't give up. Yes, we might have our disagreements, but I won't lose hope!" I said, sitting down next to her.

"What? You like me?" she asked, shocked. She looked at me as if she were going to kill me with her eyes.

"Not in that way—just as a friend!" I said, fumbling slightly.

"I don't trust you. Yet, I don't know what it is about you that makes me keep talking to you!" she said, staring at me for a moment. I glanced back at her, and her expression gave me an unexpected sense of relief. Rakshit was right— her eyes said a lot. After a minute, her eyes started to twinkle.

"When you start talking with me, you'll gradually get to know me and understand why you began engaging with me in the first place. Someday, in your own time, you'll realize what it was about me that drew you in!" I said, chuckling softly.

"Are you flirting with me?" she asked.

"I don't think so. I wouldn't want to take this risk of you stopping talking to me!" I replied.

"Imagine if that happened. What would you do then?" she asked.

"Well, that's a tricky question. Honestly, I don't have an answer right now. At the moment, I just want to get to know you. That's it!" I said.

"By the way, you're quite the expert in flirting. I think you're done, so now it's my turn. I need to go study because exams are coming up, and I don't want to fail. Bye!" she said, standing up.

"Not fair. I have to admit, you're quite smart!" I said.

"Well, thank you. I'll take that as a compliment!" She said with a smile as she began to walk away.

"At least tell me when we'll meet again!" I asked.

"We're at the same college, so we'll run into each other more often. Let's see when that happens!" she said, raising her eyebrows.

"I'll be waiting!" I said.

"Believe me, you should concentrate on studying instead of on me!" she said.

"Well, that can be decided later. Bye!" I replied.

She walked away with a smile. She was right about one thing—I definitely needed to buckle down and focus on my studies with the exams just around the corner.

NOTES

I got so wrapped up in chatting with Ahana that I completely forgot Professor Jain's first lecture was today! Being late to his class was always risky; if you are tardy, you have to face a barrage of tough questions throughout the lecture. Professor Jain had two major pet peeves: students arriving late and any gossiping. His class was known for its pin-drop silence. Somehow, I managed to get there before he did.

"Where have you been? Why are you late?" Ethan whispered in my ear.

"I got stuck!" I kept my answer short to avoid any more questions.

"Stuck? Where?" he pressed on. One of Ethan's habits that often annoyed me was his persistence—once he latched onto something, he wouldn't let go until he got a satisfactory answer.

"Can we discuss it after the lecture?" I suggested.

"What are you two gossiping about? We'd like to join in!" Professor Jain interjected sarcastically. Everyone turned to look at us. It felt as if they had just discovered the key to escaping the monotony of the lecture.

"Excuse me, Sir, I've been instructed to sit in this class from now on!" Ahana said. Seeing her made me feel unexpectedly happy, though I couldn't quite understand why. For now, she was my rescuer.

"What's your name, Miss?" Professor Jain asked.

"Ahana Sharma!" she replied.

"You should have been here a week ago. May I ask where you've been until now?" Professor Jain inquired.

"I was in the library, compiling my notes. If I had shown up with incomplete notes, I would have struggled to keep up. I've tried to cover as much of the course as possible. It won't happen again; I'll attend every lecture from now on, Sir." she explained cleverly.

"I hope that's true. Now, please take a seat, Miss Ahana!" Professor Jain said. Every boy in the class was staring at Ahana, and I couldn't help but feel a pang of jealousy.

"Welcome to our kingdom, 'Jangli Billi.' You're free to hunt here, dear." Ethan whispered.

"I'm here for the rules, not the hunt, but thank you for your emperor, I'll keep it safe!" she replied.

"Do I need to get an auspicious time set for you to sit?" Professor Jain scoffed.

"Sorry, sir. I'm just going to sit now!" She said as she took a seat next to Hazel.

My focus drifted from Professor Jain's lecture to Ahana, who was immersed in her studies. I wasn't feeling quite right without teasing her, so I jotted down a note and sent it to her.

How much will you read?

Vihan

She read the note and glanced at me. After a moment, she passed back a note with the following message:

As much as it takes to stay focused.

Her smartness was impressing me.

Now that you're my classmate, so let's be friends.

Don't say no.

I waited for her response, but she remained silent. Eventually, my patience wore thin, and I gave her chair a gentle nudge with my foot. Finally, she responded.

What are you doing?

Do you enjoy being punished or something?

I was actually enjoying myself, so I wrote another note and sent it to her.

I love to tease you and will keep doing so until you become my friend.

The choice is yours!!

This time, Hazel read the note as well and gave me a sly smile. I had a feeling something fishy was brewing in her mind.

You can't give me a choice. I am the master of my mind.

Her replies were so clever that I thoroughly enjoyed our conversation.

Let's see then. I like challenges.

As soon as she saw my note, she quickly wrote a response and tossed it back to me:

Same here.

I didn't feel right bothering her too much, especially since even talking in Professor Jain's class felt like a dream. I didn't want Professor Jain to scold her because of me. I read all her notes again, a smile creeping across my face as I did. While I was engrossed in one of her notes, Ethan grabbed the rest, read through them, and giggled. Rakshit also read the notes and gave me a sceptical look. For the first time, I wasn't sure how to react.

SAPIOSEXUAL FRIENDSHIP

The pressure of exams is consistent whether you're in school or college. I can't speak for everyone, but I liked the exam days. The campus looked like a book fair with everyone carrying their textbooks. That was the scene during our first year—no one knows how it will be by the time we reach our final year. I always have fond memories of exam days. It seemed like we invented countless ways to study, each with its own unique "funda." I won't go into details about our particular methods—after all, boys often have their own "logic-less" approaches. The movie 3 Idiots is a testament to that!

I was eagerly waiting for the exams to end so I could finally have a proper conversation with Ahana. The exam frenzy made it almost difficult to catch sight of her—she seemed to vanish into her own 'Magic Land' during the exam days, a place where no one could find her. I hardly ever saw her outside of class and had no idea where she went for the rest of the day. Was she always this studious, or was she just catching up due to her late admission? I realized there was no point in overthinking it, so I decided to wait for her on campus.

"Why are you standing here?" Rakshit asked.

"Hey! I was lost in thought and didn't notice you arrive, sorry!" I replied defensively.

"May I know what were you thinking so deeply that you didn't even see me standing here?" Rakshit pressed.

"Hey, thanks for the notes. Are you waiting for me?" Ahana interjected.

"Whoa... when did you get here?" I asked, taken aback by her sudden appearance. She had just saved me from Rakshit's intense interrogation, making her the real hero of the day.

"Just appeared before you," she replied with a hint of mischief. "Can't you see, or should I say, I just stepped out of Narnia?" She raised an eyebrow, her tone playful.

"Do you enjoy dodging straight answers, or is it just a habit of yours?" I shot back, my curiosity piqued.

"Keep asking dumb questions, and you'll get answers to match!" she retorted, rolling her eyes in exasperation.

Just then, Rakshit chimed in with a chuckle, "By the way, you handle Vihan's silence quite impressively!" He was clearly amused.

I shot him a narrowed gaze, "You seem to be enjoying this a bit too much, Rakshit."

Ethan, seemingly confused, asked, "Did I miss something?" while exchanging a knowing wink with Ahana.

"So, you're back in the jungle, Mr. Trickster!" Ahana said with a smile. I stood right before her, but she treated me like a ghost - invisible and nonexistent. It's infuriating, feeling like I don't exist in her eyes. She always ignores me, and it's frustrating.

"Thank goodness the exams are finally over, but did you hear that Shreya and Dhruv are dating now?" Hazel said, sounding anxious.

"When did you start working as a flatterer? Your talent won't go to waste—I'll make sure of it. I promise, don't worry." Ethan said, causing everyone to laugh. He was always eager to pull someone's leg.

"Anyway, I don't get what Shreya sees in Dhruv. I don't think he has anything special about him, I don't see why she'd like him. But it's their business, let it be." Ahana said with a glazed look.

"He's the most handsome guy in college after Vihan!" Hazel said.

"Grow up! He's just good-looking, but... he doesn't have much going on upstairs. Looks don't work everywhere—it's the mind that matters. I'm surprised you believe in looks!" Ahana said, clearly shocked.

"I don't, I'm just saying!" Hazel replied quietly.

"Oh, come on... sometimes a person can be wrong, and I guess you count as one, it happens, Hezu!" Ethan said with a chuckle.

"Why don't you stop teasing her?" Rakshit scolded Ethan.

"I'm not bothering her. Ask this 'Jangli Billi.' Don't let me down—you're my only hope, don't betray me." Ethan said, winking at Ahana.

"Your antics have gone on long enough. Let's go! Ethan, you'll find more people to tease in class, we'll get a fifteen-day vacation starting tomorrow, and today is the last day." Rakshit said, and he, Hazel, and Ethan started walking away.

"Aren't you two coming?" Rakshit asked me and Ahana.

"I'll be right there!" Ahana replied.

"No, she isn't. I have some work with her, so we'll catch up later, you guys go ahead." I said quickly.

"Can I join?" Hazel asked.

"I think you've watched '3 Idiots' a bit too much, my Hezu. Uniforms don't work everywhere. Let's go!" Ethan said, and we all laughed.

"Why did you stop me? What do you want?" Ahana asked, her tone flat and uninterested.

"Nothing important, but you mentioned you don't value looks. So, what do you value?" I asked.

"Of course, it's the mind. You stopped me just to ask this?" she replied, rolling her eyes.

"Not exactly. Can't you have a peaceful conversation for two minutes?" I requested.

"OK, fine!" she said, clearly irritated.

"So, you like someone intellectually stimulating, right?" I asked.

"Not necessarily a genius, but I'm the kind of girl who's attracted to sapiosexual people!" she said.

"Can I ask why?" I inquired.

"It's the mind that has the solution to everything, it's it simple?" she said, raising her eyebrows.

"Don't you think the heart has some solutions too?" I asked, moving a little closer to her.

"I... I've got to go now, What... what are you doing?" She said. I could tell she was a bit nervous from my proximity.

"Alright, just tell me if I have a mind or not?" I asked.

"Why? Don't you know yourself?" she asked.

"I do, but I want to know because I need to ask you one more question based on your answer. So tell me." I said.

"Where are you coming up with all these questions? Tell me, where exactly is your questionary factory?" she said sarcastically.

"First answer my question, I'll tell you." I insisted.

"Alright, fine. It seems like you have a mind, The way you keep arguing with me makes me feel like that." she giggled.

"So, if I have a mind, that means you might consider being friends with me?" I asked.

"Well, I'm still not interested but you make a point." She said with a smile.

"Please, agree! Believe me, it won't be a lost deal, we'll catch up after fifteen days. I can't wait that long." I sighed.

"Friendship is never a loss or a profit! You've already tried your best, what's next?" she asked.

"I don't know how to convince you, it's tough to win you over!" I said quietly and she laughed. Her laughter transformed her face, making her beauty shine brighter. The sweet sound of her joy resonated deeply with me. It was a rare moment of connection, as she typically reserved our conversations for study-related topics only. I couldn't help but wonder why she kept me at arm's length.

"Ok, fine. Give me these fifteen days to think about it and don't give me that puppy look!" she said.

"Full vacation? Who thinks that much about friendship?" I asked, shocked.

"I do. I'll consider it when I have some free time, and why would you assume I'd spend my entire vacation on that?" She said with a playful tone.

"Seriously? Alright, I'll give you fifteen days, but for me, you're already a friend, and I'm counting our relationship as a friendship. It's all up to you now." I said while looking at her.

"Correction: It will be a sapiosexual friendship, Mr. Vihan!" she said, laughing.

"As you say! I think we should head out now, let's go." I said, and we both walked away.

I was hoping these fifteen days would pass quickly. I had accepted the idea of friendship, but I was sure about her—she could surprise me at any moment! She seemed to operate on her terms, never asking for permission before making a splash. Each time I encountered her, she found a new way to surprise me. I couldn't wait to see how she'd surprise me after the break.

NONNA

The thrill of coming to college made me feel like my life would be full of freedom and happiness. But as soon as I stepped into the hostel, I was missing home within seconds—especially when faced with the bland, mild, and overly acidic hostel food! Honestly, I didn't miss home that much, but the hostel food made me long for it. I know it sounds selfish, but it's the harsh truth. After all, who would want to stay at home and lose their freedom? At least, I wouldn't.

After the accident, my sense of home felt diminished. It wasn't that there was a fight at home, but I missed my sister dearly. My room was a constant reminder of her; she used to spend the entire day there. I'm unsure who was responsible for the accident, but my mom still maintains that no one was to blame that day. Maybe it's because mothers are always inherently altruistic, which is why they hold such a revered status, but I still don't like it. It's not that I think what they did was wrong, but I don't understand why it seems that people only truly appreciate someone when they're no longer in this world. I can't understand this phenomenon.

Time seemed to play tricks on me, and its favourite game felt like 'peek-a-boo'! I never really enjoyed vacations much. I was constantly reminded of Jiya, and the accident left me with countless questions swirling in my mind. At home, old memories lingered, making me feel haunted, so I preferred to stay at my grandmother's house. I spent more time there to escape those memories and found solace in her company. I know my grandmother must be aware of something about Jiya's accident. I tried to talk to her about it a couple of times, but she always insisted that no one was at fault—it was just an accident. She used to advise me to forget the accident as if it were just a nightmare.

I used to call my grandmother lovingly Nonna. I chose to enroll in college in Jaipur partly to be near my grandmother, who lives there. After Jiah's accident, my grandmother chose to stay in Jaipur, though I'm not sure why. Whenever I visited her, she could sense that I had some issue weighing on my heart that needed addressing. Nonna knew more about me and Jiya than even my parents did. We shared everything with her, and she listened with genuine interest. We didn't used to say much but she seemed to understand everything intuitively. I don't know what kind of magic she possessed. Now, as I returned home… I was filled with confusion about whether Ahana would accept my friendship. I wondered what Nonna would say about it if she knew about Ahana.

"How are you finding college?" Nonna asked, sitting on a dining table chair.

"It's a mix of fun, reading, knowledge, logic, suspense, drama, and mystery!" I said, sitting down next to her.

"Hmm… Can I know her name?" she asked, looking at me intently.

"Name? Whose name?" I replied, stammering a bit.

"Since you arrived, it's been like you're waiting for someone. Who is that girl who keeps you so distracted?" she inquired.

"It's impossible to hide anything from you... Her name is Ahana," I said, pinching her cheeks softly. That's why I like Nonna the most.

Nona's expression turned introspective when she heard her name, as if memories were resurfacing.

Suddenly, she gasped, "Ahana!" - her name escaping her lips in a mix of shock and amazement. I nodded, acknowledging the unexpected revelation.

"Do you like her?" she asked, her smile beaming with a knowing glint. Nonna's demeanour in the past few minutes had been unnerving. I felt like she harboured a secret connection with Ahana, one that I couldn't quite grasp.

"I'm unsure if 'like' captures it, but she brings out a smile in me like no one else. I fabricate reasons to talk to her, and I'm not sure if it's because she soothes my thoughts or her words leave me mesmerized. I love teasing her, but she always retaliates with clever comebacks. There's an enigmatic quality to her that fascinates me. I've met many girls, but she's in a league of her own. Nonna, I don't know what to do?" I confessed, sighing deeply.

"What's your plan now? Are you going to pop the question?" she teased, her smile playful.

I laughed, correcting her, "Not quite. I do appreciate her clever banter and our chats, but romance isn't on the table. I've asked her to be friends, that's all." I explained, dispelling any misconceptions.

"Oh, come on... 'Get out of town'! I'm your Nonna. You might be able to hide things from yourself, but not from me. You know very well what you want. The way you talk about her is unlike anything I've seen before. Whenever her name comes up, your face lights up with a smile. I can tell you care about her a lot. I don't understand why did you asking for friendship if you love her. Why not propose directly?" Nonna said, raising her eyebrows.

"I wanted to start with a strong foundation," I explained, feeling a bit uncertain. "I've always believed that friendship is the key to a healthy relationship, so I thought it was the best place to begin..."

"It's not necessary. If your love is genuine and there's trust in your relationship, then friendship will naturally be a part of it. If you think she's a 'smart cookie,' why waste that potential on just a friendship zone? Friendship is important, but not every love needs to begin with friendship. You can be friends even after falling in love. If her presence makes you comfortable and happy, why let her go? This is a problem with your generation—you overcomplicate relationships and then complain that life is complicated!" Nonna said with a heavy sigh. I was taken aback. Nonna had seen through my feelings of love.

"I've already asked her for friendship. If I propose to her now, She might end up making things awkward for me. What should I do now?" I said with a sigh.

"Hahaha… You know what you need to do. Don't rush, you just need some courage and faith. Believe in yourself and your love, my child. Give yourself some time to understand." Nonna said, laughing.

"Nonna, are you giving me advice or scaring me?" I asked.

"I'm not sure, but I'm enjoying your situation right now!" she giggled. She kissed me on the head and headed to the kitchen.

I knew that Nonna was deeply concerned about me. Ahana's name alone could make me smile, and it was true. Her eyes fascinated me the most. The more I used to think about her, the more I wanted to see her. For the first time, I didn't like vacation, and there was still a week left. I felt as if time had stopped completely for me!

SLEEP MODE

Waiting eagerly for something, only to face delays for trivial reasons, can feel like being trapped without bars—an emotional prison. That's how I felt recently. After Nonna's insights, I realized how deeply I care for Ahana. Before her, I wasn't interested in anyone else, but... there's something uniquely captivating about her that caught my attention. I'd pondered this many times but couldn't find a clear answer. Whenever I said or heard her name, a distinct smile would appear on my face. Honestly, I was scared about how I would express my love to her, especially when I had only asked for friendship. She asked for time to think about being friends—will she need an entire year to consider my feelings? Only time will tell, or perhaps she knows!!

At that moment, I was in such bad shape that I couldn't even go to college because of a fever. I was eager to see her, talk to her, and tease her, but... my fever has ruined everything! I didn't know whether to blame my luck or my excitement. This awful fever completely dampened my enthusiasm. Now, I'd have to wait another two or three days to see her, as the doctor advised taking extra care due to the viral nature of the illness. The thought of missing out on seeing Ahana only made me feel worse. Lost in my thoughts, my phone rang—it was Ethan.

"Hi. I thought you were coming, where are you?" he said from the other end of the line.

"Sorry, I forgot to let you know, I'm feeling under the weather!" I replied.

"I thought you were just sleeping because you were tired, not that you had a fever. Why didn't you tell me this at the hostel?" he said.

"Knock, knock... my name is Alzheimer's. I already mentioned that I forgot to inform you!" I said with a touch of sarcasm.

"Anyway, I'll be there in ten minutes. Until then, just rest... and one more thing, you can't steal my sarcasm, that's my signature move! " He said and hung up.

Before I could say anything, he'd already ended the call. Sometimes I couldn't figure out what he was trying to do, like Ahana!! He will never speak directly to anyone. I'd never seen him talk to anyone straightforwardly. I was too tired to think about it, so I drifted off to sleep. After a while, I heard some noises and knocking at my door. Along with Ethan, Rakshit and Hazel were also at my door!

"Hey, guys!" I said, clearing my throat.

"It looks like you were taking a cat nap!" Hazel remarked.

"I was... but what are you all doing here?" I asked.

"Rakshit wants to start his company here and has come to fill you in. So, I hope you would have time to listen." Ethan said, his sarcasm evident. My condition was so bad that I couldn't grasp anything he said, including his sarcasm.

"You're such a bad egg, Ethan!" Ahana said. I was shocked to hear her; it came completely out of the blue.

I could hardly believe that Ahana had come to see me! I didn't want to ask why she was here, because Ethan would likely respond in some unexpected way. It still felt like a dream that Ahana was standing in my room.

"Ignore him. Get some rest, and don't worry about the notes—I'll make sure you get them, Vihan!" Rakshit said.

"Considering how you're feeling right now, I don't think you should focus on your studies now!" Hazel added, nodding.

"I'm just not in the right state, I don't feel much of anything, I want to sleep!" I said with a scoff.

"Love and fever are both strange ailments. Despite all the feelings in the world, you can't feel a thing!" Ethan remarked.

"One more shot and you're out, I swear!" Hazel said, clearly annoyed.

"Shh... he's trying to sleep. Could you lower your voice?" Ahana said.

"I'll take these two out, Ahana, you stay here. Ok." Rakshit said, leading Ethan and Hazel out with him.

"How are you feeling now?" Ahana asked.

"Honestly, I'm not feeling great, and I feel sleepy… I guess probably because of the medication." I said, glancing at her.

"Where's your phone?" she asked.

"It's on my wardrobe, over there!" I replied, pointing.

She stood up, retrieved my phone, and started doing something with it.

"What are you doing?" I asked.

"Just adding my number to your phone…" she said. "If in case you need anything, you can call me." She then sat back down next to me.

"Why do you care about me?" I asked.

"I thought about our friendship zone and… you're not that bad. So, as a friend, I should take care of you!" Ahana said with a smile.

"I don't want your friendship right now!" I replied.

"What?" She asked, shocked.

"Yes. I want all of you, not just half of you." I said while looking at her.

"I think you need to rest, what are you talking about?" she said.

"I wanted to clear up your confusion today, but my poor health kept me in the room, sorry for that!" I said with a sigh.

"We're running late. Ahana… let's go." Hazel said.

"I'll be there in two minutes!" Ahana replied.

"I'll let you know if I need anything, you should go, Ahana!" I said with a smile.

"Just make sure to rest properly and call me if you need anything, okay?" she said and hugged me.

"Did you just hug me?" I asked, surprised.

"Don't be conservative; Friends can hug each other, it's pretty common. What the big deal in it?" she said, raising an eyebrow.

"Of course, I'm not... but I didn't expect it from you!" I said surprisingly.

"I hope you get well soon, and one more thing… don't tell me what you expected. I don't like to follow anyone's expectations!" She said with a smile before heading out.

Her words were always used to confuse me. Sometimes she said things that were hard to appreciate. I don't think she would have ever spoken directly to anyone! Sometimes, both Ethan and Ahana were getting on my nerves.

DAYDREAM

The fever had worsened my condition for two days. Ahana had given me her number, but I was so ill that I couldn't bring myself to call her. Both of my days were quite strange, as the fever made me feel awful, and on top of that, I was feeling weak. At that time, having Ahana's number seemed pointless. I was barely aware of anything and constantly sleepy. After a few days, as I started to feel a bit better, once again, Ahana consumed my thoughts. I couldn't stop replaying the image of her hugging me. Though my fever made me too foggy to notice what she wore that day, she looked stunning!

I was incredibly frustrated when Ahana came to see me, and I couldn't even talk to her properly. I couldn't believe I had missed such a great opportunity! Plus, my luck seemed to be working against me, as right after I started recovering, the exam dates arrived, and we were all busy with preparations. This made it quite difficult to find time to talk to Ahana. The saying "It never rains but it pours" I felt like it perfectly described my situation. I wanted to meet Ahana privately but struggled to find the right way to ask her. I kept staring at her number on my phone, considering calling her, but I couldn't bring myself to do it. On top of everything, I was confused about how to express my feelings to her.

"What about you, Vihan?" Hazel asked.

"Huh?... Hmm... about what?" I replied.

"I don't think you're paying attention!" Hazel said, looking at me.

"He's still bummed out about missing the farewell party and all the hot chicks. I can understand your feelings, Vihan!" Ethan chimed in with a laugh.

"I'm not interested in the party. Besides, I don't think I should be part of any gatherings now. I've just recovered and don't want to risk getting sick again. I want to stay out of it." I said seriously.

"You're right!" Rakshit agreed.

"That may be true, but Ethan, did you really like those girls? None of them seemed particularly smart." Hazel said,

"Well, they might not have had brains, but they had looks, we all know. Girls can't always have both, can they?" Ethan replied with a wink at Hazel. Rakshit and I tried hard not to laugh.

"You're lucky Ahana isn't here!" Rakshit said with a grin. "Otherwise, she'd give you an earful about this. Don't you remember what happened with Hazel last time?"

Ethan chuckled. "Of course, I remember. Poor Hazel." He playfully pinched Hazel's cheek.

"Hope I didn't miss anything!" Ahana asked, entering the conversation. She wore black shorts and a canary-yellow long-sleeve T-shirt. Today, she looked different—maybe the ponytail or the earrings. Every time I saw her, she seemed to have a new quality that caught my attention. I couldn't quite figure out why.

"Well, not much!" I said, glancing at her.

"Glad to see you!" Ahana said with a smile.

"I'm feeling hungry. Does anyone want some snacks?" Ethan asked.

"You're such a glutton. You just had Lay's chips!" Hazel said, eyeing him suspiciously.

"No, no, no—don't give me that look. And, by the way, they were just chips! Haven't you heard that chips are light?" Ethan protested.

"Hey, you guys don't know? Ethan is on track to break the world record for gluttony and get his name in the Guinness Book!" Ahana said sarcastically, and we all laughed, except Ethan.

"You're all laughing at me now, but I'll have my revenge later!" Ethan said.

"It's time to feed your 'stomach-house', I guess you should go, dear!" Ahana replied.

"Wait, we're coming too!" Rakshit said.

"I need to talk to Vihan, you guys go ahead, will catch you later!" Ahana said. Now this came out of nowhere!

"Don't you think you two are spending a lot of time together lately?" Hazel remarked with a hint of sarcasm.

"Come on, stop overthinking. You're supposed to come with me, aren't you?" Ethan said, pulling Hazel along with him.

"By the way, she wasn't lying at all!" I said, looking at Ahana.

"People say what they see. If they misinterpret things and speak out of turn, that's on them. We can't control what others think." Ahana replied, raising an eyebrow.

"Mistake? I don't see it that way. My feelings for you aren't a mistake." I said seriously.

"What? What are you talking about? It sounds like the fever is still affecting you. Have you lost your mind?" she said, stepping back.

"Oh, come on! Set aside that nonsense. You know you feel something for me too, so why the denial?" I said, trying to convince her.

"Who said I have feelings for you?" she asked promptly.

"If you don't, why did you hug me that day? I was sick, but I could see the concern on your face. Sure, friends worry about each other, but why did you give me your phone number? I live in a hostel with Rakshit and Ethan—if I needed anything, they could have taken care of it. The way you looked at me, it's clear that no friend looks at another friend like that. It was my fault for asking you for friendship in the first place. You have feelings for me, but you're not admitting it. I don't understand why?" I said confidently.

"Cut the crap. I don't believe you. I don't know why you're saying all this misleading stuff today. If you need something in the middle of the night, the warden will not let you out. I only gave you my number because I'm at home and you're in the hostel. My purpose was only to help you." she said.

"If your health is bad, they'd let you go anywhere for medicine at midnight. I thought you knew that!" I replied sarcastically.

"I'm getting late, bye!" she said, but I pulled her closer, gripping her wrist firmly.

"Your heartbeat is getting faster, I don't understand why you're refusing to admit this, but your eyes clearly show that you have feelings for me?" I asked.

"The positive and negative terminals of a battery connected with a low-resistance conductor, causing a short circuit in my heart. Now, tell me that's not true?" she said sarcastically and tried to free her wrist.

"I'll make you believe you have feelings for me, I won't give up!" I said softly.

"Honestly, don't audition for drama, you'll be rejected. That's such a cheesy and cliché line!" she said and smiled.

"You're good at changing the subject!" I replied.

"Don't you think you're wasting time on this?" she said.

"Aren't you just changing the topic or avoiding the issue?" I said, stepping closer to her.

"There's nothing like that... just let go of my hand. Can you stop coming toward me like that?" she mumbled the last part, avoiding eye contact.

"Okay, one day you'll come to me and admit you love me!" I said, finally letting go of her hand.

"We'll see. Overconfidence isn't great either!" she said, rubbing her wrist.

"I love my life!" I replied.

"What?" she asked.

"Once you study the 'Love' chapter, you'll get it, It's beyond your understanding right now...but don't worry, I'm good at teaching." I said, kissing her cheek. I still felt like I was dreaming about kissing her cheek, even though it was real.

"What the hell! How dare you? How can you kiss me without my permission?" she said furiously grabbing my collar.

"Hahaha... and you say you don't love me? You're upset because I kissed you without permission, but you're not even mad about the kiss itself!" I said softly, smiling.

"You're crazy, I hate you!" she said, releasing my collar.

"I'm glad I won over you today," I said softly.

"Count it as your reward!" she said irritatedly.

"What's the use of a reward that doesn't bring you happiness?" I retorted.

Ahana teased me, "Some prizes are valuable only in name." We both left the canteen.

FORMULAS

From what I knew about Ahana, she would never accept her feelings for me that easily, and I was fully aware of that. She was perfect for me, but if she were to agree too easily, it wouldn't be as fulfilling. Achieving anything, whether it's a goal or love, requires effort. The happiness you gain from something you've worked hard for far exceeds that of something you get effortlessly. So, a little effort should be worthwhile. It was hard for me; a year and a half had passed, yet she still wasn't ready to admit that she had feelings for me in her heart! Now, I don't know how to persuade her.

To figure out if Ahana had feelings for me, I decided to employ a few tried-and-true methods. I tied a handkerchief around my left leg and started walking with a slight limp. I made my way from campus to the canteen with my unusual walk, and only a few people noticed and asked about it. I should win an award for acting—pretending to walk like that and maintaining a fake expression as if something terrible had happened wasn't easy. Acting is incredibly challenging, but I perceived it today.

"Hey, what happened to your leg? Did you hurt yourself?" Ahana asked. Thank God I kept limping, or I might have been caught!

"Just tell me, don't you have a magic wand? Where do you come from?" I asked in shock.

"Shut up and tell me what happened to you!" she demanded. Her concern for me was evident in her eyes.

"It's nothing, just a little cut. I'll be fine within a week." I said, putting on a pained expression.

"What? How did it happen?" she asked quickly.

"We were playing volleyball last night at the hostel. I must have injured it there. I found out this morning when I started having pain... but don't worry I'll be alright soon!" I explained. I couldn't believe I was coming up with stories like this!

"But why is this handkerchief tied like that? Opt for a bandage instead of a handkerchief—it's safer and helps reduce the risk of infection. Honestly, I recommend that you see a doctor as soon as possible." she said, examining my leg.

"Whoa! Don't tell me you're studying both engineering and Pharmacy!" I replied with a wink.

"You're unbelievable! You're hurt and still in the mood to joke around!" she frowned and walked away.

I just wanted to confirm whether she cared for me, but she left without saying a word, clearly upset. Did I make her angry? I had a strong sense of unease and didn't think any of my tricks would work on her. I was lost in thought, sitting on the stairs. Honestly, my feet were aching from walking like that. I was busy looking at my feet when a girl from my class approached and stood beside me.

"Hi, what happened to your leg?" she asked.

"Nothing... it's just a little scratch!" I sighed. I felt frustrated that the person I went through all this drama for had left without a word.

"Oh! Well, I have a bandage if you need it!" she offered kindly. I wished Ahana had approached me this way.

"No, thank you for asking but I'm fine though!" I replied with a smile.

"Let me know if you need any help. Okay?" she said. I noticed Ahana approaching with a bandage in her hand. Seeing the bandage in her hand, I confirmed that she at least cared for me. I wanted to hug her, but it was time to move to Formula No. 2.

As soon as Ahana approached us, I began talking to the girl.

"Actually, Thank you so much for your concern. I think your bandage will help me." I said to the girl.

"Oh, it's nothing. Here, take this. Hope you will be fine soon!" she said, handing me a bandage with a smile. I glanced at Ahana out of the corner of my eye; she seemed quite upset with my antics. She tossed the bandage she had brought for me into the trash and walked away. I couldn't help but laugh internally, though I also felt a bit sorry for Ahana.

Later, I went to the canteen, where Ahana was with our group. Everyone was looking at me with curious expressions, especially Ethan.

"So, how long has this been going on?" Ethan asked with bright eyes.

"What are you talking about?" I replied, confused.

"Oh, come on. Ahana told us everything. Why didn't you mention it? How long have you been dating Riya?" Hazel asked.

"What? Who's Riya?" I asked. I couldn't make sense of anything. I looked at Ahana, bewildered, but her smirk confused me more.

"Ahana saw her giving you the bandage. So don't play dumb." Hazel said.

"Oh! There's nothing like what you're thinking, guys. She just gave me a bandage, that's all. Believe it or not, I only learned her name from you, Hazel. Why did you assume that we were dating?" I asked, looking around at everyone. Everyone then turned to look at Ahana.

"Based on the way you spoke to her, I assumed she was your girlfriend!" Ahana said, looking down.

"Wow! May I know who you are? I've seen something like this in the movie Aparichit—they described multiple personality disorder, or it wouldn't be wrong to say that Hazel is influencing you." Ethan said sarcastically, and everyone laughed except Ahana.

"I just said what I felt, so just shut up!" Ahana said, her voice tinged with anxiety. I found her face so innocent, if I had my way, I would hug her right before everyone.

"Stay away from Hazel. It's tough enough handling one detective; how would we manage you too?" Ethan said, and Rakshit and I laughed along with him.

"Why am I even involved in this?" Hazel asked, fuming.

"I'm sorry, Ahana... but this time Ethan is right. If someone talks to someone for just two minutes and you immediately label them as a couple, that's something Hazel would do. Now you're acting the same way!" Rakshit said with a chuckle.

"It's all my fault or misunderstanding—whatever you all choose to think. I'm sorry. Ok? Ahana said, standing up.

"Where are you going?" Hazel asked her.

"I don't know, but I'm not in the mood to stay here!" Ahana replied furiously.

"It's like a once-in-a-blue-moon event for me. For the first time, I've seen her this angry!" Ethan said in astonishment. I was equally shocked, like Ethan, to see this side of Ahana.

"Indeed! She usually responds with a comeback. Why did she get so upset today?" Hazel asked, surprised.

"Not again! Don't always play detective. She's human too. Sometimes people get angry, and it's not a big deal!" Rakshit said politely.

I didn't expect it, but all my tricks worked surprisingly well. She didn't admit it, but it was clear that she was jealous when she saw me with Riya. I could see both anger towards me and jealousy towards Riya in her eyes. Now, there was only one formula left. I took out my phone and sent a text to Ahana.

I haven't told anyone anything.

Meet me at the rehearsal hall after college today.

Just for 5 minutes—I promise.

I love you.

Five minutes later, I texted Ahana again immediately.

Sorry, it wasn't for you. Ahana.

I don't know if she saw my text, but if she did... I'm sure she would have shown up at the rehearsal hall. If she shows up, I will take it as a sign that there's a place for me in her heart and that she loves me too.

THE WRONG DICE

I sent Ahana a text, but I wasn't sure if she would come to see me. I didn't even know if she'd read my message! Honestly, this was my last attempt. I was feeling quite confused because, after the way she left the canteen, I wasn't sure if she would show up. Still, I decided to wait for her. Knowing her, she disliked procrastination and was always punctual. Based on that, I arrived at the hall ten minutes early before she came. I was searching for a spot to hide because I wasn't sure how Ahana felt about me. All the moves I was making were based on speculation. I had no idea if she had any feelings for me at all. I chose to hide near the entrance, where boxes were stacked on the right side. It was an ideal hiding spot because if Ahana didn't show up, I could easily slip away through the entrance.

I wanted to see what fate had in store for me. I loved her deeply, and though her attitude drove me crazy, I couldn't deny that destiny plays a role in such matters. You can achieve a lot with luck, but while hard work and courage are also important, we often end up attributing success to luck. In the end, it feels like destiny is what truly determines our path.

I glanced at my watch—it was five o'clock, but no one had arrived yet. I decided to wait a bit longer. I was anxious, worrying about how I would explain myself if someone else showed up at the hall. To make matters worse, this was the first time I had missed Professor Jain's lecture. What was gnawing at me the most was why Ahana hadn't shown up yet. From what I knew about her, she was always punctual. I was also worried that my plan might backfire and overwhelm me, which made me increasingly tense.

It was 5:15, and Ahana still hadn't arrived. My hopes were sinking, and it felt like they were drifting away. I had hoped she would show up, but now I was beginning to think she might see me as nothing more than a good friend. It was a painful truth, and accepting it was more difficult than I had imagined. I quietly moved the boxes aside and started to leave. Just as I was about to open the hall door, Ahana walked in with friends.

I couldn't grasp why she had come to meet me along with everyone else.

"I thought you would be in the disciplinary office! Our college is like a magical land." Ethan gave me a sarcastic look.

I stared at Ahana in surprise, but she showed no expression at all. There was something odd about her behaviour.

"What are you all doing here?" I asked, a bit hesitantly.

"I was supposed to have 'bhaji-pav' today, but now it feels like I'll have to go to Bombay to get it. I heard someone from Bombay would come to make that delicious dish!" Ethan said sarcastically. I often wondered why he never just answered a question directly.

"Stop bothering him. Anyway, Vihan, how long have you been here, and why didn't you attend Professor Jain's lecture? You didn't even send a text. For some reason, Mr. Jain seemed to miss you a lot today. So, what are you doing here?" Hazel asked. She threw so many questions at me that I didn't know where to start in answering them.

I stood there in silence, feeling as if all my senses had shut down. I couldn't grasp what was happening. I had been expecting Ahana alone, but now everyone was with her. The way they questioned me made me sure that Ahana hadn't shared anything with them. At the same time, I was confused about whether she had read my text or not.

"I was feeling down, so I went to lie down here. I forgot to mention it to you all, sorry for that." I said, trying to handle the situation as best as I could.

"Is everything okay? Is something bothering you? You can share with me if you want to." Rakshit said, placing a hand on my shoulder.

"Thank you, but there's nothing like that at the moment. But what are you all doing here?" I asked again.

"Nothing special. Mr. Jain asked us to leave a few things here, so we helped out. We didn't expect to find you here. I still don't understand why you're here!" Hazel said, clearly surprised. It was becoming difficult to handle Ethan, and now Hazel acted like a detective too. Before I could answer her question, I noticed Riya approaching us.

"What is she doing here?" I asked, looking at Riya in surprise. Everyone else turned to look at her as well.

"This is a college; anyone can go anywhere," Ahana replied sarcastically. I couldn't tell if she was angry or jealous. Honestly, I wasn't in a position to understand much at that moment.

"Wow, that's a nice shot, Ahana!" Ethan said, winking at her. Sometimes, I do not like when Ethan flirts with her.

"Shut up, Ethan! Riya was free, so she also offered to help us." Rakshit said.

"Hi! Oh, Vihan, there you are! Mr. Jain missed you a lot today in the lecture." Riya said with a smile. I glanced at Ahana, but she seemed indifferent.

"You'll be on the news tomorrow—better give me an autograph now. Who knows? Maybe tomorrow you'll claim you don't know any of us!" Ethan said, mocking me. Riya looked a bit disappointed after hearing Ethan's comment. Rakshit shot an angry glance at Ethan. After a moment of silence, I decided to break the tension.

"By the way, I forgot to ask—what's all this?" I asked, trying to lighten the mood.

"This is just some stuff from Mr. Jain. He mentioned that he'll show us something here next week, I'm wondering what?" Hazel explained.

"I think Mr. Jain has lost his mind. This isn't a lab but a Rehearsal Hall!" Ethan said.

"Why are you always so quick to make fun of someone?" Rakshit scolded Ethan. "Maybe he would be planning to do something else instead of practical work."

"We'll find out next week. But I can't stand all this stuff anymore. I'm tired." Ethan said, and he headed inside the hall with the luggage.

Everyone else followed him to put the items away. I kept glancing at Ahana, trying to figure out if she had read my text. I was also hoping for a chance to check her phone to see if she had seen my message, but such an opportunity wasn't presenting itself. I couldn't muster the courage to talk to her. While everyone was busy organizing things and chatting, my gaze kept drifting to Ahana's phone repeatedly. My mind was a blank slate, and Ahana's usual behaviour was only adding to my frustration. I was so confused that I couldn't think clearly. I don't know how to approach her now. Will she even want to talk to me?

LIBRARY

I expected Ahana to read my SMS and that I'd be able to express my feelings, but things didn't go as planned. My efforts backfired and now I was ashamed of whatever I did. Since that day, I haven't dared to speak to Ahana. Whenever she was around, I remained silent, overwhelmed by embarrassment over my 'SMS thing'. I often planned to clear up the misunderstandings by talking to her, but whenever I got a chance to talk with her, I would freeze and be unable to say a word. It was really difficult for me to accept that she only saw me as a friend. Since that day, I've been avoiding eye contact and maintaining as much distance from Ahana as I can.

Professor Jain had scheduled a seminar in the hall. As I walked in, I felt embarrassed and found myself muttering under my breath. I couldn't concentrate on the seminar at all. The only thing that caught my attention was the equipment my friend and Riya had brought; nothing else seemed to capture my attention. In the end, I came up with an excuse to leave and headed to the library to find some tranquillity. I was sitting on the bench with my eyes closed, enjoying a moment of peace, when Rakshit came and sat down beside me.

"Do you want to say something, or should I start questioning?" Rakshit asked with a smile.

"I didn't realize you were so perceptive!" I sighed.

"I'm good at many things, but right now, I'm curious about why you're avoiding Ahana. What happened between you two?" Rakshit asked, looking surprised. I explained everything to him, and he laughed. My actions were so childish that I felt ashamed of myself, so it was only natural for him to laugh. Before he could say anything further, Ethan and Hazel arrived as well.

"I'm telling you, something's off!" Hazel said to Ethan. Rakshit and I exchanged puzzled looks, unsure of what she was referring to.

"If there's a problem, just ask him directly. Why are you arguing with me about this?" Ethan said, clearly irritated.

"What are you two talking about?" Rakshit asked, looking confused.

"Don't you notice anything?" Hazel demanded immediately.

"Miss Hazel, I don't have a mind like yours, and I'm not a detective. If this suspense game is over, could you please tell me what's going on?" Rakshit replied.

"Don't you really know?" Hazel said, giving me a curious look. "Maybe it's just me, but I feel like something's different in you Vihan."

"What are you talking about?" I asked, puzzled.

"He thinks you have a girlfriend and are hiding it from us!" Ethan said, sounding uninterested.

"Maybe you should find a new hobby. You're watching too many detective shows nowadays, Hazel." Rakshit teased.

"Seriously? You always jump to conclusions. Can you explain why you think that?" I asked, clearly irritated.

"Why do you always pick on me? Can't you find someone else to bother?" Hazel snapped angrily.

"You know the answer, don't you?" Ethan said.

"Will you two be quiet? You both keep bickering every time. Remember, we're still in the library." Rakshit said, scolding them.

"So, we can go outside and argue, then?" Ethan asked with a grin.

"Talking to him is like pouring water on a stone, he will never be going to change. Trust me." Hazel said, rolling her eyes.

"You're no better than him. Honestly, neither of you deserves any praise. Every time I look, you're just trying to outdo each other. Can't you see the extent of the animosity between you two? Is this good?" Rakshit said angrily.

"I have no interest in fighting with him. I don't want to waste my time." Hazel said.

"Ya sure. I enjoy it when I get a headache and by the way, what are you doing right now?" Ethan said, not looking at Hazel.

"Who told you to stick your nose into my business?" Hazel shot back immediately.

"And you never do anything about me, do you?" Ethan retorted.

"Are you two going to be quiet or not?" Rakshit said angrily. "If not, get out of here before I lose my temper."

Noticing Rakshit's anger, they both quietly exited the library. I had never witnessed Rakshit so enraged before today.

"Now tell me, what are your true feelings for Ahana?" Rakshit said, turning towards me. Seeing Rakshit's anger, I realized I had to provide a clear and direct answer to his question.

"I've met many girls, but she's different. Her way of speaking reminds me of Ethan, yet she's the only one who can truly quiet me..."

"I wasn't asking about Ahana's qualities. I need a straightforward answer: yes or no, that's it." Rakshit interrupted.

"Yes!" I said, complying before he could get any angrier.

"Listen carefully," Rakshit began. "What you did was certainly childish, and we can't put this off any longer. You know this is our final year." He sighed before continuing.

"I understand what you're trying to say, but I lack the courage to talk to Ahana after what happened. I can't even face her!" I replied, feeling devastated.

"If you really care about her, don't let her go. Yes, she may speak her mind, but she is pure by heart. Take all the time you need, but when you're ready, let her know how you feel." Rakshit said and patted my back.

"Thank you for your support. I'm planning to introduce him to my grandmother, perhaps she could offer me some advice." I sighed.

"That's a good idea. It's been a while since we saw her anyway. We can all visit your grandmother under that pretext." Rakshit said quickly. I was relieved to see that his anger had finally subsided.

After a while, he left the library. I called my grandmother and informed her that we'd be coming home next week. From her response, it seemed she was happy about the visit. My main concern now was figuring out how to persuade Ahana to come to my grandmother's house.

CONSEQUENCES

I agreed with Rakshit's suggestion and decided to share my feelings with Ahana. I thought my grandmother might offer valuable advice, so I included everyone in my mission and planned a visit to her house. Although it was challenging to evade Ethan and Hazel's inquisitive minds, it wasn't my main concern. The real challenge was convincing Ahana. I was too nervous to speak with her directly, but Rakshit intervened and successfully convinced her to join us.

"I still don't understand why we're suddenly heading to your grandmother's place?" Hazel asked, clearly sceptical.

"Grandma kept all the celebrities at her place just for you, don't you know?" Ethan teased, poking fun at Hazel.

"Don't you two ever get tired?" I asked.

"No, because this is my identity after all!" Ethan said with pride.

"Where? In hell? Break a leg!" Hazel retorted, causing everyone except Ethan to burst into laughter.

"It doesn't matter if my identity is in hell," Ethan continued with a smirk. "But you, on the other hand, don't even have that identity. Want to know why? Eh, don't ask. I'm happy to answer. Even in hell, there would be people like us, so if you tried to bring your loyalty and spying into the mix, it would just spoil our fun. And don't even think about heaven, because you're not loyal to yourself! So, I doubt you'd make it there either. You might want to consider where you truly belong. I know it's a serious question."

We all struggled to hold back our laughter. Poor Hazel! Ethan always has a counterattack, leaving Hazel with no choice but to stay silent.

"Can you two stop bickering like cats and dogs? You've been at each other's throats for three years, constantly roasting each other. Don't you ever get tired of it?" Rakshit asked.

"I don't think it'll make any difference to either of them. Some things just need time. When the right time comes, they'll both calm down." Ahana said with a smile.

Rakshit and I followed Ahana's advice and waited for the cab to take us to Grandma's house. After a short while, the cab arrived, and we reached Grandma's place within an hour. She was overjoyed when I told my grandmother that I was bringing my friends over. According to her nature, she would be busy making new dishes at home for us. Grandma has a magical touch in the kitchen and still cooks for herself. Her passion and resilience are truly inspiring. Cooking has become her hobby. I still don't understand why she chose Jaipur. Nothing seems to be exceptional about it. I rang the bell, and after a moment, Grandma opened the door. The instant she opened the door, a delicious aroma filled the room, making my stomach growl with hunger.

"What are you cooking? It smells amazing!" I asked eagerly.

"I thought you'd ask about my health first!" Grandma said with a smile.

"I know you're always so absolutely fine. I apologize, but the incredible smell from your kitchen drew me in before I could even say hello." I said and hugged Nonna.

"Let us all have a chance to meet Grandma too. Are you going to greet her alone?" Rakshit said with a smile. Except for Ahana, everyone else had a turn to greet Grandma individually. Ahana was on the phone.

"I saw you all in the first year of college when Vihan brought you all home, and now I see you again today. What can I complain about? Your answer will be the same—studies kept you busy! By the way, where's that special friend of yours?" Grandma asked teasingly. As she finished her phone call, I introduced her to Ahana.

"Nonna, meet Ahana!" I said with a shy smile.

"Why are you blushing like a girl?" Ethan whispered in my ear. I shot him an annoyed look.

Ahana said hesitantly, "You... in this... city?" Looking at my grandmother in surprise. We were all taken aback, as none of us had known that Ahana was acquainted with Grandma.

"You claimed Ahana didn't know your grandmother, but it looks like you were the one who betrayed us!" Ethan said dramatically.

"I already suspected something was off, but who listens to me?" Hazel added.

"Will you two be quiet? I don't know anything myself. I'm also clueless." I said, defending myself.

I looked at Ahana and noticed she seemed a bit serious. But why would she be nervous around my grandmother?

"Vihan doesn't know anything about it, so don't bother him with questions, he doesn't know anything!" Grandma said calmly.

"Then how do you know Ahana?" Rakshit asked.

"Are you all going to stand around outside, or are you coming in?" Grandma said, then turned and went inside.

We all followed her, with Ahana's face still showing confusion. I wanted to ask Grandma how she knew Ahana, but as soon as we went inside, she headed straight to the kitchen.

Soon, a variety of delicious dishes appeared on the dining table. My friends and I helped set everything up. Grandma had prepared an impressive spread: Handi Biryani, Tandoori Roti,

Paneer Makhani, and Samosa Chaat for starters. I was amazed at how she managed to prepare all these dishes, even at her age. For dessert, she had made Ghevar, a beloved Rajasthani treat.

Everyone was enjoying the meal, but I was too distracted to eat. I couldn't wait any longer and asked Grandma during dinner, "How do you know Ahana? I recall during our conversation when I mentioned Ahana's name, your expression seemed to change a bit too. Was there something you weren't telling me?" Everyone looked at Nonna and Ahana. Grandma kept silent for a few minutes, gazing at Ahana, who looked nervous.

Nonna said with a mocking tone, "You think I can confirm it's the same Ahana just because of a casual conversation? You haven't shown me a single photo, even the best detectives can't identify someone based on a brief chat. So, how can I be certain it's really her?" The room erupted in laughter, with everyone except Ahana finding the exchange amusing. Ethan, in particular, seemed to be enjoying the teasing.

My mouth hung open in mock astonishment at Nonna's cheeky remark. I shook my head, and

THE DIARY

went to Nonna's house seeking advice, but I ended up more confused than ever. There was no clear solution to my problem, and my confusion only grew. I couldn't understand what troubling Ahana was, but she seemed even more unsettled after meeting my grandmother. I can't stand secrets, and it felt like I was caught in a web of riddles and hidden truths. On top of that, Grandma's words unsettled me even more. Her words kept replaying in my mind, and I couldn't shake the feeling that Nonna was hiding something from me. I tried to bring up that matter with her a few times, but she always dodged the topic.

I never expected my last year to turn out like this! My year had been going very poorly. I used to hide from Ahana, but now it felt like she was avoiding me. Whenever we were with our friends, she either didn't show up or stayed for a short while. Sometimes, it was just the two of us, but I failed to start a conversation with her, despite all my efforts. Sometimes she would call and ask to meet, but then she wouldn't show up or would be unable to talk. I was completely baffled about what was going on in her mind!

We were all hanging out in the parking area, chatting, though I wasn't very invested in the conversation. As usual, Hazel and Ethan were arguing with each other again.

"This year will be over soon, and who knows when you'll see each other again. At least try to get along for the next six months, without causing any more trouble to each other." Rakshit said, trying to convince them.

"It's not a piece of cake dealing with him!" Hazel said with frustration.

"What's the fun in something easy to get?" Ethan teased Hazel. "Don't you think?"

"It's pointless to argue with them, let it go!" Ahana said. I looked at her and tried to figure out what she trying to hide from me.

"What are you staring at?" Ethan teased me, causing everyone to turn and look.

"Why are you targeting him now?" Hazel snapped. "Sometimes it seems like you're a hunter who's become prey yourself and now you're just shifting your focus to someone else!" Hazel barked.

"Don't use metaphors if you don't know how to use them, my dear Hezu!" Ethan said with a chuckle.

"What do you mean?" Hazal asked immediately.

"I wish I were a vampire!" I blurted out suddenly, causing everyone to look at me in surprise.

"Since when did you start drinking blood?" Ethan asked, his tone irritating me. I stayed silent, which made him more uncomfortable.

"What's wrong? I've noticed you've seemed a bit down for the past few days." Rakshit asked.

"I'm fine; it was just a slip of the tongue!" I replied, feeling frustrated.

"Well, at least you didn't say you wanted to build Antilla since that's impossible!" Ethan said mockingly, but everyone around me shot him angry looks.

"There's no point in trying to read someone's mind. No one knows that vampires are real or just imaginary." Ahana said, leaving everyone as astonished as I was.

"Everything else feels irrelevant when you're searching for a solution!" I said quickly.

"Even if we don't want to...sometimes we should wait for the right moment, that's it!" Ahana said a little bewilderment.

"Timing isn't the issue, it's just that our situation is already set." I countered.

"You're not wrong, but it's too related to timing!" Ahana said. Everyone else looked at us, perplexed.

"I didn't know we were still in high school!" Ethan interrupted, causing us all to look at him in disbelief.

"What? How long have these two been discussing 'Time'? At school, we often engaged in debates like that or were given assignments on similar topics." Ethan said, clearly irritated.

"There's no need to be annoying. But I also don't understand what's going on. You both seem different these days." Rakshit said seriously.

"It's nothing like that... I'm alright." Ahana said hesitantly.

"I'm just preoccupied with a small project these days. I'm fine too." I said, trying to reassure Ahana. She gave me a small smile, but it seemed forced.

"You two aren't at odds but you support each other well. Not bad at all." Hazel said with a wink.

"Not everyone is like you, right?" Ethan shot back, roasting Hazel again.

"Don't you have anything better to do?" Hazel snapped angrily.

"I'd rather study. If any of you want to come, feel free. to join me" Rakshit said as he started walking toward college. We were all laughing at Ethan We were all laughing at Ethan because he missed the chance to roast Hazel.

I noticed that Ahana seemed to want to say something to me. I was about to muster the courage to approach her when she suddenly turned and started walking away, causing a diary to fall from her bag. I picked it up and intended to return it to her, but she vanished when I looked up. I didn't want to read but I couldn't control myself. I opened the diary and saw her name on the first page. I read a couple of pages while standing there, but I found it was a personal diary, I stopped and put it away.

Instead of going to college, I went straight to the hostel. Once there, I examined her diary, unsure whether I should read it. One moment, I felt I shouldn't invade a girl's personal space, while the next, I questioned whether it would be right to read it. Conflicted, I decided to start reading her diary. At first, I found it intriguing and engaging. As I kept reading, I found something that answered all my questions and made me feel both angry and upset. Overcome with emotion, I threw the diary against the wall in frustration.

APOLOGY

For days, I kept noticing to see if Ahana would say anything to me, but she remained silent. She seemed even more upset than before, and I understood why. I was growing frustrated but managed to keep my composure. I hoped she would eventually come to me and explain to me by herself, but she didn't utter a word. My patience was running out, yet I gave her several opportunities to communicate with me. However, her behaviour suggested she had no intention of bringing it up.

I decided that if she didn't give me any information about Nonna's meeting and the incident with my sister within two days, I would go to her myself and ask about everything. On one hand, I was frustrated with her. On the other, I was angry with myself for loving someone who didn't appreciate anyone's feelings. A deep restlessness gnawed at me, leaving me feeling unsettled. I went up to the college roof and sat there, seeking some reprieve. I held her diary in my hand, repeatedly asking myself whether Ahana would have come forward with the issues if the diary hadn't been discovered. I asked myself if I was wrong to read it and whether she was genuinely innocent or just pretending to be naive. Lost in these thoughts, I was interrupted by a call from Hazel.

"Where are you? I need to talk to you about something important. Please don't take this lightly or as a joke. I need to see you right away." Hazel said, her voice filled with nervousness and worry. I told her to come to the roof of the college, and soon after, she arrived at the terrace, gasping for breath as if she had run all the way there.

"Why did you run away like a criminal?" I asked, offering her my bottle of water to drink. After she took a drink, she returned the bottle to me. Her gaze landed on Ahana's diary. Her eyes widened, and she seemed even more distressed as she looked at it. I was puzzled by her reaction.

"Why are you looking at this diary?" I asked Hazel.

She replied, "I'm curious about why you have it. Have you read everything in it?" Her questions made me feel like she already knew more than I was. I stared at her in surprise.

"Did you know about this too?" I demanded, my anger boiling over.

"Listen, Vihan... I didn't know anything until last night. Ahana said everything to me last night, and that's why I'm here to explain to you." Hazel said, trying to calm me.

"She can tell everyone else, but not me. How could she do that? And why are you the one here to explain, not Ahana?" I said with anger.

"She told me yesterday that she would explain everything to you today. She's been in a dilemma, and it wasn't easy for her to keep this from you. She's been crying since last night. She didn't keep this from you intentionally. If she had, she wouldn't have shared everything with your grandmother that day. I understand your anger, but I think... you should give her a chance." Hazel said gently.

"It doesn't matter; she should have come to me first not you!" I said, still fuming.

"Vihan!!" Ahana called out. I turned to look at her. Her face was marked by restlessness, her eyes were swollen, and her expression reflected deep distress.

"Why were you pretending to be ignorant when you already knew everything? Do you take pleasure in playing with other people's feelings? I think you and your sibling are cut from the same cloth. My sister isn't here today, and now you are also to blame for my sister's death." I said, my anger intense.

"I also lost my brother. It was an accident, but I still feel responsible." Ahana said, her face filled with sadness.

"What are you doing in my life now? What do you want from me? Are you trying to kill me too?" I asked in anger.

"Vihan! Do you have any idea what you're saying?" Hazel scolded.

"His anger is understandable. If I were in his position, I'd probably react the same way. It's alright, Hazel." Ahana said softly.

"Don't pretend like you care about me!" I said irritated.

"What's happening here?" Ethan asked. Rakshit also was with him.

"Why do I feel like something serious is going on? Why do both of you look so shaken?" Rakshit inquired.

"That day was my brother's graduation ceremony, and we held a party to celebrate the occasion. It was the first time I met her. My brother was deeply in love with your sister. During the party, I had the chance to meet your sister and quickly learned that she had a genuinely pure heart. Every conversation she had seemed to revolve around you and Nonna. Honestly, her praise made me eager to meet both of you. After the party, both wanted to drop me at home, but I insisted they go alone. I still regret that decision. They were in the front car together, while I was in another with my driver behind them. In a split second, my impulsive decision to drive myself home proved disastrous. I convinced my driver to let me take the wheel, but my confidence was short-lived. As I sped down the road, I lost control... and my car hurtled towards my brother's vehicle. I accelerated instead of braking, and the impact sent his car spinning. The trailing car crashed into us, and the consequences were catastrophic. My brother and Jiya suffered unimaginable pain, while I escaped with mere scratches. The weight of my recklessness crushes me - I took their lives, and I still can't explain why I lost control that fateful night." Ahana's body shook with sobs, and Hazel's gentle touch offered a comforting solace. "Why did my grandmother let you go?" I asked, despair evident in my voice.

"As soon as I regained consciousness in the hospital, my first thought was to ask about my brother and your sister. But I was so badly injured that I could barely stand. I mustered the strength to get to the door, but as soon as I opened it, your grandmother saw me and had me put back in bed with the help of the nurses. Despite my repeated requests, no one would let me see my brother. During that time, your grandmother learned everything about the accident and consoled me." Ahana said, wiping away her tears.

"What did she tell you?" I asked, still angry.

"I shared every detail of the accident with your grandmother, reliving the horror of that night. Despite her own pain, she comforted me, insisting

I wasn't to blame. But I felt compelled to own up to my actions and go to the police. Your grandmother, however, cautioned against it, urging me to focus on the present rather than dwelling on the past. She believed revealing the truth would only lead to more suffering, without changing the outcome. I understood her perspective, but my conscience ached to confess to your parents. I'm tormented by the thought of what I've done, and I can only hope for forgiveness." Ahana's voice trembled as she spoke.

"Hell with your apologies. Fuck with your apology, I don't want it. Save it for yourself!" I snapped, my anger was clear in every word.

"Vihan! Watch your language. Ahana isn't to blame for what happened. It was an accident!" Rakshit scolded me.

"It doesn't matter whose fault it was. I lost my sister because of this bitch!" I said, my voice broke.

"Vihan!... I..."

"Don't you dare to take my name with that filthy mouth of yours, you whore." I interrupted Ahana.

"Vihan, you are crossing your limits now!" Hazel shouted in frustration.

"We understand you're upset, but please don't use abusive language towards Ahana!" Rakshit told me.

"We understand your pain, but why are you directing your anger at Ahana? Take a moment to calm down and you'll see that she's not at fault for the accident, Vihan." Ethan added, placing a hand on my shoulder.

"No... none of you understand the pain I'm in right now. Please leave me alone. Go away, I don't want to talk to anyone right now." I said, folding my hands in frustration and angrily returning Ahana's diary. They took Ahana away, and I sat alone on the roof, crying.

GENIE

Since that day, everything between Ahana and me has changed. I never thought I could hate someone I love so deeply. Even after our argument, the group's dynamic shifted. Everyone was upset with me for the inappropriate things I said to Ahana. Hazel, in particular, was furious, because I had crossed a line that shouldn't have been crossed. Despite this, my friends understood my situation and were willing to talk to me rather than stay angry. I regretted what I had said to Ahana, but I couldn't accept that I had lost someone so dear because of it. I felt nothing but pain, trapped in a confusing and difficult situation.

Ahana tried every possible way to get me to talk to her. She texted, called, and spent hours in the library every day. Convincing me had become part of her daily routine. She attempted some sorts of strategy to engage me, but I remained unresponsive. Sometimes, she would wait outside my hostel for hours, but I ignored her. She sought excuses to join me in class and the canteen, but I never gave her a chance. Every half-hour, my phone buzzed with her apologetic messages. Frustrated by her persistence, I changed everything she knew about me, including my phone number. After countless attempts and no success, she finally gave up.

I never imagined my last year of college would turn out like this. I had envisioned us spending it together memorably and fantastically. Instead, the reality was that we were drifting apart rather than growing closer. Everyone else remained the same, but the rift was between Ahana and me. I understood their predicament, as they were friends with both of us. Choosing sides was as challenging as preparing for the GRE. Ethan's sharp sarcasm that neither Ahana nor I wanted to involve him in our conflict. Rakshit, with his calm demeanour, could handle any problem with ease. And Hazel—she was the only one left to deal with the fallout of our issues. She often found herself in the middle of our troubles. Poor Hazel!

Everyone was discussing their project ideas in class. Professor Jain was set to review the projects and explain how they could become a powerful tool for our careers during campus interviews. While everyone else was anxious about their projects, my main concern was avoiding having Ahana as my partner.

"So, is everyone ready?" Professor Jain asked us.

"Yes, Sir!" we all replied in unison. It felt like we were back in kindergarten.

He went around the room, asking each of us about our projects and pairing us up accordingly. Within fifteen minutes, he had formed groups with more than half of the class. I was anxiously waiting for the professor to ask about my project before anyone else's but, he started with Ahana.

"Miss Ahana, could you describe your project a little?" Professor Jain asked her.

"Sure, Sir. My project is called the 3-Phase Supply Phase Sequence Checker. It involves feeding a 440V AC 50Hz 3-phase supply into a logic circuit made up of NAND and OR gates to detect the phase sequence of R, Y, B. A monostable 555 timer is triggered to monitor the sequence. If the sequence is incorrect, the timer's triggering is missed, which is indicated by an LED driven from the 555 timer's output. If the phase sequence reverses, a tripping signal is generated from the NAND gate and the 555 timer. This tripping signal is then sent to a PLC, microprocessor, or relay circuit to protect the system from reverse phase sequence. That's the basic concept." she explained.

I couldn't believe that my project was so similar to hers!

"According to this, Vihan is the right partner for your project. I believe Vihan has a good grasp of the subject. If you work together, I'm confident you'll both be well-prepared for the campus interviews and maybe even get selected for their company!" Professor Jain said while looking at me and Ahana.

"Thank you, Sir, but may I request a change of partner?" I stood up and asked.

"Yes, Sir. I also don't think he's suitable for this project. May I change my partner too?" Ahana added.

"Excuse me? I'm perfectly capable. I just don't want to work with you, that's all!" I replied angrily.

"Sir, please assign me another partner. I can't work with someone who is constantly angry. If this continues, I'll end up focusing more on managing their temper than on the project, which I can't afford right now." Ahana said with a hint of pride

"I don't want to work with someone who constantly seeks out conflicts. Who knows when their mood might change and ruin my project? I can't deal with that." I said coldly.

"Sir, I will work with anyone but him, I can't handle him." Ahana declared fiercely.

"Please assign me another partner. I don't want to waste my final year on this, Sir!" I said, frustrated.

"Anything else, my Masters? Your wish is my command, after all! I seem to have forgotten that I'm your genie. Please forgive me!" Professor Jain said mockingly. Laughter erupted in the class when he said.

"Silence! Why is everyone laughing? This isn't a stand-up comedy show. Both of you are engineering students, so act like it. Show some maturity and responsibility toward your careers.

Stop fighting like children. I'm not here to run a marriage bureau where you can demand your preferred partner. This is an engineering class. What I've said is final, and there will be no changes. Do you understand?" Professor Jain scolded. Despite his reprimand, the class continued to giggle.

"Okay, Sir!" Ahana and I said quietly.

"Stop murmuring. Speak up!" Professor Jain commanded.

"Sorry, Sir!" Ahana and I responded together.

"You two are excellent students. I've known both of you since the first semester, and you've always excelled in your studies and maintained exemplary behaviour. In the past three years, I've never received any complaints or noticed any mischief from either of you. I don't understand why, despite your maturity, you're arguing over something so trivial today. One more thing... resolve your issues and start working on the project. Now, sit down, both of you!" Professor Jain said.

We both took our seats. Professor Jain continued asking the remaining students about their projects. The students around me began gossiping, and their words only fueled my frustration. Ethan and Rakshit tried to calm me down, but despite their efforts, I was most frustrated with my luck. I couldn't figure out how I would complete the project with Ahana.

SILENCE BYE

Ahana and I began communicating about the project. To reduce our conversations, we divided the work between us. We used to gather all the project notes once and addressed any queries weekly, rather than tackling them daily. Working together was as challenging as solving complex mathematical equations. We would discuss our questions in the same week and try to resolve them together. Ahana was sharp in her studies, so her questions were highly relevant and likely to be asked during the project.

Only Ahana and I knew how we managed to complete the project. While I was out gathering materials, she used to work on the project. When I used to return with the rest of the materials, she focused on the theoretical aspects, and I continued with the practical work. Sometimes, we had to stay up all night to keep the project running. We took care of every detail, listing everything related to the project. This included identifying potential faulty parameters, considering possible issues that might cause the project to fail, and evaluating its pros and cons. We used to thoroughly study and research both the advantages and disadvantages of our project. We frequently tested the project to understand its limitations and took necessary precautions to address any issues.

At the same time, we had to prepare for exams. This was the last semester of our engineering; our situation was worse than that of stray dogs. There was no time for eating or drinking—only study, study and study! The pressure started from every direction: family, relatives, and professors, each adding their demands. It felt like the constant whistle of a pressure cooker and echoed the fear of failing in our final year. With only a few days left for the exams, the college resembled a library, with students studying everywhere, even in the canteen. Seeing the freshers having fun made us, the final-year students, envious. At the same time, it was a stark reminder that our days of carefree fun were going to end and that a new era of responsibility was about to begin.

The exam stretched two weeks, followed by a campus interview a week later. During that week in between, we began our submissions. It felt like everything was in chaos, with our minds overwhelmed by one exam after another. The last few days seemed like we were about to marry our engineering textbooks! Along with the books, we started dreaming about three-phase induction motors, vernier calipers, synchronous generators, substation layouts, cathodes, single-phase wires, and more!

Everyone was on edge, wondering if they would cut the interview. Everyone wanted to set their lives on the right path and contribute to their families. The campus interview was a crucial opportunity to soar to new heights. Each year, top companies come to hire the best candidates. To make a good impression, we dressed meticulously and groomed ourselves carefully. Along with a polished appearance, having solid practical knowledge was crucial. It was clear that understanding real-world applications was just as important as grasping theoretical concepts. The interview questions frequently centred on practical scenarios and real-world knowledge.

Everyone aimed to perform their best, as this was a golden opportunity that no one wanted to miss. Fortunately, everyone in our group received job offers.

Today was our last day together. Starting tomorrow, everyone will head to their respective homes, and we don't know when we'll see each other again. The pain of parting with friends is overwhelming. On the first day of college, we barely knew each other, but by the end, our friendships had grown so deep that the thought of separation brought tears to our eyes. Those who were strangers at the start of college have become so dear to us that the idea of leaving them feels like a void inside. The memories of mischief, fun, and laughter we shared brought tears to our eyes. The connection we'd built over the past four years had deepened so much that it now felt like family. On the first day of college, we wondered how we'd get through the next four years, but today, we were amazed at how quickly time had flown by. School days are cherished, but college friendships are truly priceless. I don't know what the atmosphere at the Farewell Party will be like.

"What's your plan?" Ethan asked Hazel.

"Nothing. Why do you care?" Hazel replied, sounding annoyed.

"Whoa, take it easy. Why are you so upset?" Ethan asked, surprised.

"Ethan, she's missing Ahana. Just leave her alone." Rakshit said gently.

"But she's coming to the party too, right?" I said confidently. Everyone looked at me with confusion, their silence charged with awkwardness as they avoided making eye contact.

"What's going on?" I asked.

"Oh, it's nothing. Anyway, what's your plan?" Ethan said with a forced smile.

"Cut the secrets. What are you all hiding?" I pressed.

"It's about Ahana...And I don't think you'd want to hear anything about her." Hazel said softly.

"So what? It's the last day of college. You guys can talk about whatever you want. If Ahana shows up, I'll find somewhere else to go, just chill." I said, shrugging.

"You won't need to do that, don't worry!" Hazel said sadly.

"What do you mean? Is she coming as a ghost or something?" I asked, amused.

"Nice joke, but bad timing, dude!" Ethan said quickly. I looked at him, puzzled, while Rakshit shot me a frustrated look.

"Fuck you, you bloody asshole. What do you want to hear? Do you have any idea how our last year was destroyed because of your fucking pointless fight? Ahana turned down a fantastic offer because of you. You were both hired by the same company... but as soon as she found out about you, she withdrew her application. And now, she's gone home today without saying bye to us! You have no clue about her pain. You branded her a murderer, hated her, fought with her, humiliated her every day, made her cry, and made her life miserable. What the fuck do you think, Vihan? How long do you think she could have carried the weight of that guilt? You only thought about yourself and never considered what she was going through. You have never tried to grasp her situation! Everyone makes mistakes and deserves a chance to apologise. You punished Ahana for something that wasn't her fault! She didn't cause the accident that day, nor ask your grandmother to remain silent. If you ever take a moment to think, ask yourself why she told your Nonna the whole truth even knowing the consequences would be severe. She could have stayed silent, but she chose to tell the truth to your grandmother, not realizing the harsh punishment she'd face for it. You should have listened to her and given her a chance to explain." Hazel said, wiped away her tears and stormed out angrily.

"This time, she's right. Anyway, enjoy the party!" Ethan patted my back and went after Hazel.

"I won't say much, but if you realize what you've lost, you should do everything you can to reclaim it. I hope you come to understand its value someday." Rakshit added before leaving as well. And just like that, I was left all alone at the party.

"Here you are! I've been searching for you everywhere. Why are you sitting here all alone?" Rakshit said.

He wore a peach-coloured kurta that paired perfectly with his off-white salwar. I still couldn't believe he's going to get married tomorrow! I was sitting in the farthest corner, lost in old memories, and hadn't even noticed how alone I was.

"Honestly, I was just reminiscing about college days!" I said with a smile.

"That's nice to hear. What was your favourite part?" he asked, sitting beside me.

"I'm not sure, but now I understand what you meant on our last day of college!" I replied with a touch of regret.

"I'm glad you remember my advice. It's still not too late—this is a great chance. Express your feelings before she moves on. She loves you just as much as you love her." Rakshit said with a delightful smile.

"I don't know how to talk to her. How can I face her knowing that I hurt her deeply? Everyone, except me, knew that she loved me. I couldn't understand her feelings, and I ended up pushing her away when I tried to express them. Now, how can I confess my feelings to her? Even if I try to express my love now, will she even acknowledge it? If I truly loved her, I should have listened to her back then, but I was too caught up in my desperation and sadness that I failed to see her pain. Over the years, I've questioned whether what I did to Ahana was right. My heart always knew the answer, but my ego prevented me from accepting it. Hazel was right—my ego had become so overpowering that I ignored Ahana's pain and kept humiliating her, while she endured it all in silence. I'm filled with anger and disgust toward myself now." I said with a heavy heart.

"The most important thing is that you've realized your mistakes. Your regrets are significant, and the situation can still be corrected. Now, regarding Ahana, tell me... how much have you moved on in these five years?" Rakshit asked.

"What do you mean?" I asked, surprised.

"It's been five years—why do you still have feelings for Ahana?" Rakshit replied, raising an eyebrow.

"What kind of question is that?" I said perplexedly.

"Listen, whatever happened five years ago, your mistakes were significant. You were deeply hurt and ended up making some regrettable choices. Your anger led you to ego and then to hatred. Amidst all this, you failed to see that she was in pain and still trying her best to reach out to you. Now, you have the chance to bring her back into your life, why do you want to let it slip away? Do you think Ahana can love anyone else but you? I don't believe she can. For God's sake... don't let her go this time." He said, trying to convince me

"I don't like this habit of you guys! Didn't I warn you that gossiping isn't allowed? It seems like everyone is gossiping except me! I didn't expect this from you, Rakshit!" Ethan said, glaring at him and reprimanding him.

"We're not gossiping. I'm just explaining something to Vihan. You're being such a drama king!" Rakshit retorted.

"Marriage tips, really? It's your marriage, not his! Naughty boy, Vihan! Have you secretly tied the knot? When did this ship sail?" Ethan said, amused.

"Can't imagine how your girlfriend deals with you!" I said, astonished.

"I don't take girls seriously, but they sure take me seriously!" Ethan replied with pride.

"Exactly... That's why no girl has managed to stay in a relationship with him." Hazel laughed. Rakshit and I both chuckled softly.

"Oh, you know a lot about me! I hope you're not stalking me, stalker! How's your detective business going? Not doing too well? By the way, movies and web series are all over Netflix and Prime these days. Watch those... you might learn something for free. Plus, it could help you revive your business." Ethan said mockingly.

"I don't understand how any girl would be interested in you?" Hazel said, exasperated.

"It's pretty simple! Not all girls are spies!" Ethan replied, and everyone laughed except Hazel.

"I shouldn't have bothered talking to you!" Hazel said in frustration.

"You know how he is, so why even try to cross him?" Rakshit said with a smile.

"Will you ever behave yourself?" Ahana asked, twisting Ethan's left ear.

"Ouch, Mom! Easy!" Ethan said, and everyone burst into laughter.

"You'll never change!" Ahana said with a smile. Her smile still mesmerized me. It was hard to catch a glimpse of Ahana with Hazel's watchful eyes constantly on me. Why does her spy-like instinct never seem to rest?

"If you'd be willing to be my girlfriend, I'd be more than happy to be a good boy for you!" Ethan said, winking at Ahana.

"I'll deal with you later. Right now, I need to talk to you, Rakshit!" Ahana said, nervously.

"Sure, what's up?" Rakshit replied.

"I've been trying to book a cab, but I'm having no luck!" Ahana explained.

"Why do you need a cab?" Rakshit asked.

"I need to head out for a bit!" Ahana said.

"Honey, that's what he said. You don't need to book a cab—I can drive you wherever you go." Ethan said anxiously.

"Yeah, I know, but I'd rather not go out with you!" Ahana replied, and we all chuckled softly.

"Don't worry, it's not a date. You girls always seem to think I'm up for one!" Ethan joked.

"Just ignore him. Vihan's driving is good and will help you out. Right, Vihan?" Rakshit said, giving me a subtle nod to agree.

"Uh, yeah, I ... I can. If you want." I stammered. Everyone turned to Ahana for her response.

"Okay, I'll be ready in five minutes!" she said, walking away without looking back. As Ahana left, Ethan gave Hazel a playful pinch.

"What the hell!! What the hell are you doing?" Hazel said furiously.

"I wanted to check if this was a dream or reality, but I see it's real!" Ethan said as he sat next to me. Rakshit and I laughed. Poor Hazel always ends up being the target of Ethan's jokes and sarcasm. Ethan was eyeing me suspiciously.

"What?" I asked Ethan.

"You two are not playing a trick on us again, are you?" He leaned in closer, and I pushed him back.

"No, and I'm not gay... so don't get any closer!" Hazel laughed while I said.

"Just ignore him. Take this chance and get her back in your life!" Rakshit said, giving me a supportive hug.

"Please don't do anything foolish this time!" Hazel added with a smile.

"Shall we?" Ahana asked me.

"Ya... sure!" I replied.

Like Ethan, I was in a bit of a daze. I didn't expect her to say yes, probably forgetting that Ahana always had a knack for surprises. I glanced back at my friends, who were wishing me good luck.

THE MOMENT

I was just as stunned as everyone else—none of us expected Ahana to agree so easily. She walked ahead of me, and I followed closely behind. I was trying to figure out how to start a conversation with her while she was engrossed in her phone, completely oblivious to my presence. I felt as if I was invisible to her, like 'Mr. India'! Today, I experienced firsthand what it's like to be ignored without reason. I had treated her the same way in the final days of college, ignoring and insulting her without cause. Her ignoring me in those two moments felt troubling... I couldn't understand how she had managed to endure my past hatred until now.

We were sitting in the car, but neither of us was speaking. She occupied the front seat next to me, perhaps aware that sitting in the back would only prompt conversation. I should admit, she was just as sharp today as she was back in college. I often found myself glancing at her, but she kept her gaze fixed out the window. An awkward silence filled the space between us. While I concentrated on driving, my attention also kept drifting to her.

We sat in silence for ten minutes, and though I knew I needed to speak to her, the awkwardness between us left me at a loss for words. She sat beside me, yet I struggled to look at her directly. There was a time when I avoided her, and now I yearned for just a glimpse of her. I was consumed with thoughts about how to bring her back into my life. Inside, I felt a tumult of unease, pain, and discomfort. This was a rare chance to talk to her alone, so I summoned the courage to break the silence.

"Um... why do you want to go to the coffee house at this hour?" I asked nervously. I waited for her response, but she remained silent. After a moment, I tried again.

"Ahana, I'm talking to you. Why aren't you answering?" I asked, glancing at her.

"You wanted to come with me, and I agreed to that, but I didn't agree to talk!" she replied, still focused on her phone.

"Look, Ahana, I understand you're upset. About what happened that day..." Before I could finish, she cut me off.

"Stop the car!" she said.

I stared at her, surprised. "What?"

"I said, stop the car. The café is just five minutes away. I'll walk from here." she said, not meeting my gaze.

"I can drop you there!" I offered quickly.

"I'd prefer to walk...Thank you for the lift!" she said.

"I know that saying sorry can't heal your wounds. I realize I was cruel back then, but I lost my temper, and the circumstances made it hard for me to see your pain." I said, taking a deep breath.

"Does it even matter now?" she asked.

"Ahana, please stop it. I'm asking for one more chance. Can you give me that?" I pleaded.

"Seriously, Vihan? I was also asking for a chance. Did you ever give me that last opportunity? No... you didn't. I tried everything to explain myself to you, but you kept ignoring and humiliating me. I used to come to your hostel to talk to you—do you know how the other boys looked at me? I hoped that eventually, you would understand and accept my apology... but you embarrassed me every day, and I endured it in silence. As time went on, your resentment grew, and I lost hope. I kept trying to make you understand my perspective, but you only continued to belittle me. If you had cared at all, you would have reached out to me. You seemed to loathe my face and even my name. It felt like you had begun to despise my very presence." She sighed deeply. Her voice trailed off. I couldn't say anything, overwhelmed with embarrassment. A tense silence settled between us.

"I longed to confess everything to your family, but your grandmother's words held me back. Yet, my conscience urged me to reveal the truth. When I overheard my parents discussing the accident, I discovered you were studying in Jaipur. Determined to find you, I uncovered the name of your college and resolved to tell you everything. After convincing my parents to let me go, I arrived in Jaipur with a mix of emotions. But nothing could have prepared me for the moment I saw you. As I gazed into your eyes, I felt an unexpected spark. I enrolled in your college, driven by a desire to apologize and make amends. Your sister's love for you was palpable, even in our brief time together. I tried to talk to you many times about the accident, but I couldn't find the right moment. On top of that, with all the exams, most of our time was consumed by studying. I knew I had to meet you, but I never imagined the weight of my secrets would crush me like this." Ahana's tears flowed like a river as she spoke.

I saw tears streaming down her face as she tried to hide them from me. Unable to bear seeing her cry, I wiped the tears from her cheeks and hugged her without asking. She struggled to push me away, but no matter how hard she tried, I held her tightly and then slowly pulled back to look at her. Her eyes were still brimming with tears. I brushed a stray tear from her face and saw that she was sobbing like a child.

I gently wiped away Ahana's tears, and she tried to pull back, but I drew her closer. My right hand cradled her waist, while my left hand stroked her hair, comforting her. Slowly, she lifted her gaze to meet mine. Our faces were inches apart, and I could feel the synchronized beat of our hearts.

Her lips grazed mine, sending shivers down my spine. I gazed into her eyes, now closed, as her breath drew me in. I wrapped my arms around her, holding her tight. She entwined one hand in my hair, while the other clutched my shirt. But then, she pushed me away. Before I could speak, her phone rang, and she tried to pull her hand free. I held firm, my grip gentle but insistent. When she ended the call, I pulled her back into my embrace, but she resisted again, pushing me away with a mix of emotions.

"What happened?" I asked, taken aback by her reaction.

"Nothing!" she said, her voice cold. "It was just a moment. It was just a moment when we got swept up and ended up unexpectedly close to you." She opened the car door, and I quickly got out to stop her.

"Hey, wait. That was 'just' a moment? Don't you feel anything for me? Don't lie—I can sense your feelings for me." I said, pushing her gently back toward the car.

"No, it wasn't anything. Maybe seeing you after so long stirred up some emotions, and I kissed you asked, "Okay, fine. How do you know Ahana, anyway?"

"Oh, it's not a big deal!" Grandma said. "I met Ahana once at a temple in Bombay. It was raining heavily that day, and she gave me a ride home. That's all there is to it." Ahana nodded in agreement. I was quiet for a moment, processing this.

"Don't overthink it. Some good people stay in our memories, whether we see them after two months or twenty years. Now, eat your food, my child!" Grandma said, gently stroking my hair.

We all finished our dinner and began helping my grandmother. Ahana spent about an hour with Nonna in the kitchen, and from the way they were chatting, it seemed like they were discussing some serious matters.

After a while, we got ready to head back to the hostel. Grandma hugged me and whispered in my ear, "Try to cherish Ahana and remember not to make hasty decisions." She then kissed my forehead lovingly.

I was puzzled by her words and unsure of what she was hinting at.

in the heat of the moment. That doesn't mean I love you. Now, let me go!" she replied, shoving me away.

"Ahana, don't do this. Life doesn't always give us a second chance. We've had this opportunity after five years." I said, following her.

"I don't want any second chance, and I don't want to decipher any signals from the universe. I've put in so much effort to move on, and I'm not willing to revisit that part of my life!" she said, quickening her pace as she moved further away from me.

"I love you, Ahana!" I shouted, and she stopped.

"I understand it's hard for you to trust me. You don't have to love or trust me, but please... give me one last chance. I promise I won't let you down this time." I pleaded, my voice trembling.

"I don't know what to do?" she said, her eyes filled with tears. "If you hurt me or leave me again, I don't think I'll survive anymore."

Before I could respond, a truck sped toward her and struck her. At that moment, my entire body went numb, and for two seconds, I felt utterly paralysed.

SECOND CHANCE

I was torn between reality and a living nightmare as I rushed to Ahana's side. Gently, I lifted her into my lap, brushing away the blood from her face. Her eyes remained closed, and the sight of her fragile form, smeared with crimson, shook me to my core. My hands trembled uncontrollably as I took in the extent of her injuries, fear paralyzing me. My mind went blank, and my body felt frozen, unable to think clearly. But one thought pierced the haze: getting Ahana to the hospital. Panic and indecision threatened to overwhelm me, but I knew I had to act.

With a newfound sense of determination, I composed myself and carefully lifted Ahana into my car. I called out her name repeatedly, but she remained unresponsive, her eyes shut tight. I quickly dialled Rakshit, my voice shaking, and begged him to meet us at the hospital with the others. Though fury burned within me towards the truck driver, Ahana's well-being was my sole priority. Yet, I couldn't let the driver escape accountability; I swiftly snapped a photo of his truck's number and sent it to Ethan. As I gazed at Ahana's fragile form, tears streamed down my face uncontrollably. I sped to the hospital, my heart racing with fear, and completed the necessary paperwork with trembling hands. Then, I waited anxiously outside the operating room, my mind consumed by worst-case scenarios.

As I gazed down at my hands, the sight of bloodstained skin sent a shiver down my spine. The horror of the accident flashed before my eyes, and my body trembled uncontrollably. Ahana's blood was not only on her clothes but also on my hands, a haunting reminder of the tragedy. My anger towards the truck driver burned intensely, and I felt an overwhelming urge to make him pay for his recklessness. Lost in these dark thoughts, I noticed Rakshit and the others approaching me, their concerned faces a stark contrast to the turmoil brewing inside me.

"How did this happen?" Rakshit gasped. Ethan and Hazel standing beside him, their faces etched with worry.

"Ahana was walking on the road, and I was trying to convince her for another chance. Suddenly, a truck came speeding toward her and hit her. After the collision, the truck crashed into a divider and ended up on its side. The driver fled the scene... but luckily, I snapped a photo of the truck. I didn't get a good look at the driver, but from his erratic movements, it felt like he was drunk or injured. I focused on getting Ahana to the hospital and brought her here as fast as I can." My voice trembled as tears streamed down my face, unable to stop.

"I've already alerted the police, and they'll track down the truck driver. This kind of accident is all too common in Jaipur—people drink heavily at night and drive recklessly as if they're handling toy cars! You must be more careful. What made you choose to have this conversation in the middle of the road? Anyway, what did the doctor say?" Ethan asked, his voice betraying a rare hint of distress. For the first time, we saw Ethan speaking directly and in a serious tone.

"Since I arrived, the doctors haven't come out of the operating room. I took care of all the paperwork and came here to wait." I replied quietly.

"Everything will be alright. Don't worry." Rakshit said, placing a reassuring hand on my back.

"Everything that happened is my fault. Am I really that terrible? I can't bear the thought of losing her again." I said, my voice breaking with tears.

"Shh … Don't blame yourself. Everything will be alright." Hazel said, pulling me into a comforting hug.

We were all waiting outside the operating room, and I was overwhelmed with anxiety. It felt like I was trapped in a tiny, suffocating room. Every couple of minutes, my gaze darted towards the operating theatre. I wanted to ask the doctor about Ahana, which made my gaze habitually drift towards the operating theatre. My restlessness was constant—I'd stand up, sit down, or pace around, unable to stay still. Nervousness had made my legs shake, and the bloodstains on my hands and clothes kept dragging me back to the accident. All I could picture was her bloodied face.

Rakshit noticed how distressed I was and came to sit beside me. "Take care of yourself!" he said reassuringly. "Everything will be fine."

"I never thought my hatred would lead to Ahana teetering between life and death. Once, I despised her, but I never wanted her to suffer like this - lying on a stretcher, covered in blood, her life hanging by a thread. When the truck struck her, I was frozen in shock, my eyes fixed on the horror unfolding before me. Everything else faded into the background; I couldn't hear or see anything but Ahana. My mind went blank, unable to process the chaos. I snapped back to reality and rushed to her side, but no matter how hard I tried to rouse her, her eyes remained shut. Her broken bracelet and blood-stained face, hair, and dress made her look like she was in a deep, peaceful sleep. As I tried to move her to my car, she felt like a lifeless doll in my arms, unable to speak or move. It was a soul-crushing experience." Tears streamed down my face as the memories flooded back.

"I understand what you're going through, but don't lose hope. Ahana will be okay." Rakshit said with confidence.

We were all anxiously waiting for the operation to be completed. Rakshit's father had arrived at the hospital, despite it being just one day before Rakshit's wedding. His father had come because

Rakshit refused to leave Ahana's side. Rakshit didn't see Ahana merely as a friend; she was like a sister to him and seeing her in this condition felt like a personal torment. Ethan was visibly stressed, a reaction I had never seen from him before. He wasn't cracking jokes or teasing Hazel; the tension was so thick that every minute seemed to stretch endlessly for everyone.

After an agonising hour, the operating room door finally opened, and the doctor emerged. Every eye in the room, including mine, was fixed on them, desperate for a glimmer of hope. I was on edge, my heart racing with anticipation, as I awaited news about Ahana's condition. A crushing sense of unease had settled over me, making my legs tremble beneath me. My anxiety had reached a boiling point, leaving me struggling to catch my breath, feeling numb, and almost paralysed by fear. The silence was suffocating, and I couldn't bear the thought of anything but positive news.

THE MARRIAGE

"So, you're finally getting married. I'm so happy for you." Ethan said.

"It's hard to believe the wedding is only a few hours away!" Hazel said with an admiring smile.

"Please, just stay here and don't go anywhere!" Rakshit said, his voice tinged with nervousness. We exchanged glances, looking at one another in silent agreement.

"Why do you keep saying it? We're not going anywhere. Just enjoy your wedding!" I reassured him.

"People enjoy weddings, but not the ones getting married!" Ethan said with a smile.

We all laughed, but my smile felt a bit incomplete. Everything was the same as before, except for Ahana's absence. It wasn't just me—everyone missed her deeply.

My eyes still well up when I recall the moments we spent together. I never imagined I would lose her like this. The doctor had kept Ahana under observation for two days. During those two days, her condition showed signs of improvement. Those two days were very challenging for all of us; each moment felt like an eternity. We were consumed by constant worry: Would there be any improvement in her condition? Would she regain consciousness? Would her health deteriorate? Might she need another operation? So many questions and doubts crowded our minds.

All our worries faded away a week later when Ahana opened her eyes. I felt as if I had conquered the world that day. The doctor had asked one person to stay by Ahana's side, and everyone urged me to be that person. Rakshit and the others waited outside. As I entered the ward, my heartbeat raced, and the accident replayed in my mind. For a while, I stood by the door, but then... Ahana noticed me and gestured for me to come closer.

Ahana lay surrounded by a tangle of medical equipment - an ECG machine, a blood pressure monitor, and a pulse oximeter - a stark reminder of her fragile state. I hesitantly took a seat on the stool beside her bed, my eyes fixed on her pale face and bandaged head. A scratch on her hand, caked with dried blood from the accident, seemed to mock me, a harsh reminder of that fateful day. As I drew closer, a wave of nervousness washed over me, its intensity unsettling. I felt my heart racing, my hands growing clammy, and my mind reeling with worst-case scenarios. The beeping of the machines and the antiseptic smell of the hospital room only added to my distress.

She could barely open her eyes, so I told her to rest. As she slept for a while, I watched her with a mixture of relief and sadness that made my eyes misty. My heart was oddly unsettled. Sometimes, she would open her eyes and smile at me, a gentle smile that seemed almost out of place given the circumstances. I struggled to comprehend how someone could be so tender even in such a situation.

The accident itself was unfolding before my eyes. Each time I looked at her, I was haunted by the image of her blood-soaked face. I couldn't bring myself to look directly at her. When she placed her hand on my hand, I looked at her gaze. Tears streamed down her face, and I gently wiped them away, tenderly stroking her forehead. I couldn't understand why she was crying so much. I managed to comfort her. Though she wanted to say something, I insisted she stay quiet.

She fell asleep again, gripping my hand tightly. I held her hand in return, my gaze fixed ahead. I also closed my eyes and fell asleep. After a while, I felt her fingers start to move, which jolted me awake. She was perfectly fine. "Vihan..." she managed to whisper my name with difficulty.

"I told you not to speak now. You should take a rest." I said, my voice filled with concern.

"I am... sorry, I ... just want you... to be happy!" She could barely speak due to her distress, so I advised her to stay quiet and rest.

I was lost in memories when Hazel snapped me back to the present. I thanked her with a gesture. We were all thrilled for Rakshit, celebrating his marriage. We all felt wonderful to be together again, wishing him all the best from the bottom of our hearts. The atmosphere was joyful, but her laughter still echoed in my ears.

"I'm sure she'll be happy!" Hazel said softly.

"Thank you!" I replied with a faded smile.

"There's no need to be sad. Remember her with love, not sorrow." Hazel said, offering comfort.

"I told her to rest, but she was so obedient that she chose to rest forever!" I said with a heavy heart.

"It's been a year... I understand your feelings, but it's time to move past the painful memories. The good moments with Ahana are still with you." Hazel gently patted my back, and I nodded.

I looked at Hazel and managed a faint smile. I celebrated the wedding with my friends, I felt a deep sense of missing Ahana. Her memory will always hold a special place in my heart. Her words still echo in my mind, and her face remains etched in my memory. I loved her with all my heart, and that love will endure.

The day Ahana left us still felt like an open wound, the pain as raw as ever. Her absence had carved a gaping void in our lives, leaving us all struggling to find our footing. Rakshit's wedding was a poignant reminder of the joyous moments we had shared with Ahana, forever etched in our memories. We had shared countless laughter-filled moments, tears, and adventures, and her loss had left an indelible scar on our lives. The bittersweet celebration was a testament to the impact she had on us, a reminder that even in death, her presence would never truly fade.

The wedding celebration continued, but my mind kept wandering back to Ahana. I remembered her laughter, her smile, and her unwavering optimism. She had a way of making everyone feel seen and heard, and her absence had left a gaping hole in our lives. I knew that I wasn't alone in my grief. We all missed her deeply, and the pain of her loss still felt overwhelming at times. But as I looked around at my friends, I knew that we would get through this together. We will always carry Ahana's memory with us, and we will continue to celebrate her life, even in her absence. She may be gone, but she will never be forgotten.

The wedding came to an end, and we all bid our farewell to Rakshit and his bride. As we left the venue, I couldn't help but feel a sense of nostalgia wash over me. We had shared so much together, and Ahana's absence had left a void that could never be filled.

Ahana... a celestial soul, whose presence was a gift, and whose memory is a treasure. Her love was a symphony of laughter, tears, and adventure, forever etched in the hearts of those who loved her. With a spirit as wild and free as a 'wild cat,' she danced through life, leaving behind a trail of glittering moments, and a legacy of love that will shine bright for eternity. Ahana... my first and last love, and will be forever in my heart, soul, and memories.